Becky's
Brainstorm

The
Twelve Candles Club

9610

Becky's Brainstorm

Elaine L. Schulte

BETHANY HOUSE PUBLISHERS
MINNEAPOLIS, MINNESOTA 55438

Published in association with the literary agency of Alive Communications, P.O. Box 49068, Colorado Springs, CO 80949.

Cover illustration by Andrea Jorgenson.

Published by Bethany House Publishers
A Ministry of Bethany Fellowship, Inc.
6820 Auto Club Road, Minneapolis, Minnesota 55438

Printed in the United States of America

Library of Congress Cataloging-in-Publication Data

Schulte, Elaine L.
    Becky's Brainstorm / Elaine Schulte
        p. cm. — (The Twelve Candles Club ; bk. 1)
    Summary: To help her mom out financially and prevent the family from moving, Becky and her three best friends start The Twelve Candles Club, a business providing child care, housekeeping, car washing, and other services.

    [1. Clubs—Fiction 2. Moneymaking projects—Fiction. 3. Christian life—Fiction.]
I. Title. II. Series: Schulte, Elaine L. Twelve Candles Club ; bk. 1.
PZ7.S3867Be   1992
[Fic]—dc20   92-15202
                                                   CIP
ISBN 1-55661-250-8   AC

To

Mary Huckstep,

a dear sister and helper

ELAINE L. SCHULTE is the well-known author of twenty-five novels for women and children. Over a million copies of her popular books have been sold. She received a Distinguished Alumna Award from Purdue University as well as numerous other awards for her work as an author. After living in various places, including several years in Europe, she and her husband make their home in San Diego, California, where she writes full time.

CHAPTER

1

*H*appy birthday to you . . . you live in the zoo . . ."

Becky Hamilton ran to her bedroom window, hardly believing her friends would sing such a baby song, and right in front of her house, too. They were probably still hyped over today being the last day of school.

She caught a glimpse of them through the leafy bushes by her window. They were trooping up the front walk: Tricia Bennett, her long reddish-blond hair gleaming in the sunshine; Jess McColl, her short, sturdy body in full stride; and Cara Hernandez, her usually shy expression full of laughter.

Should I tell them the bad news? Becky wondered. All week she'd kept it from them so it wouldn't ruin the last week of school. All week she'd pretended to be happy and excited . . . and untroubled.

"You look like a monkey and smell like one, too!" her friends sang out, then laughed wildly and pounded on the door.

They might act wacko, Becky decided, but she really liked them. To her amazement, tears pressed behind her eyes, and she suddenly wished she didn't like them quite so much.

Rushing from her room to the front door, she blinked hard. She'd have to keep on pretending tonight, too. No sense ruining her birthday pizza and slumber party.

She caught a quick glimpse of herself in the entryway mirror and checked her blue eyes. Not teary. Despite everything, she looked just fine: her brown wavy hair held down by a white headband, and her tall, gangly body hidden under a white shirt and powder blue shorts.

"Happy birthday!" they called out as they leaned on the doorbell. "Happy birthday, Becky!"

The doorbell was still ringing when she threw the door open, hoping they wouldn't sing the zoo version again. "You're telling the whole neighborhood!"

"Well, why not?" asked her best friend, Tricia Bennett. "It's not every day you're twelve years old, and it's the last day of school too." She bounced with excitement, carrying in her sleeping bag, pillow, overnight bag, and a present wrapped in blue and white paper, topped with a blue bow. "You want us to sing again?" she teased.

"You wacko! You're insane!" Becky protested, but she couldn't help laughing. She'd forget her problem for the rest of the day, no matter what. She'd simply forget it.

The girls trooped to her bedroom to dump their sleeping bags and other overnight gear, then came out carrying her birthday presents.

Jess, as usual, got down to business. "Where do we put the presents?"

"On the dining room buffet, I guess," Becky answered.

Not that they really had a dining room in their small Spanish-style house; the dining room was actually an L-shaped extension of the kitchen.

"The table looks great with those blue streamers and the vase of daisies," Jess said.

"Thanks. Mom did it last night," Becky explained, admiring the decor herself. The table looked neat with a white tablecloth, white stoneware plates, blue napkins, and the blue crepe paper streamers she'd helped her mom tape from the brass chandelier to the corners of the table. A blue and white HAPPY BIRTHDAY, BECKY! sign hung over the dining room cabinet. It was crayoned in by her five-year-old sister, Amanda, who'd *almost* stayed inside the lines.

"Happy birthday, Becky!" Cara said. She carried a small gift decorated with a huge blue crepe paper flower, which she'd probably bought just over the border in Mexico.

"Thanks! Hey, you all wrapped the presents in my favorite color. They look beautiful."

Tricia lined up the gifts on top of the dining buffet. "What do you think we are, color-uncoordinated?"

"Never," Becky answered. "Never uncoordinated and never klutzy."

"Not klutzy?!" Tricia exclaimed. "Not klutzy?"

With that, her friends started their usual klutz act. They crossed their eyes, turned their feet inward, and stumbled about wildly. "Klutz . . . klutz . . . klutz!" they chorused in weird voices.

Becky started to laugh, then clapped a hand to her mouth as another pang of sorrow hit. It seemed as if she were seeing them like this for the last time: Tricia, who knew just how to play the klutz (or anything else dramatic) and wanted to be an actress; Jess, who hoped to be an Olympic gymnast like Mary Lou Retton, and even looked like her except for her short darkish blond hair; and Cara, the shyest and sweetest, who actually was a little klutzy but had the world's most beautiful brown eyes.

Becky's lower lip trembled.

They all stopped and stared at her. "What's wrong?" Tricia asked. "Something must be wrong."

Becky clenched her fists, determined not to cry. "Nothing," she began, then said the first thing that came to her mind. "I guess I'm just feeling old."

"Old!" Jess echoed. "That's crazy! Since when is *twelve* old?"

I can't let things get heavy, Becky thought. She pulled herself together and went into a decrepit old lady act, hobbling along with an invisible walking cane. "Hello," she croaked, then added in a wavering voice, "Don't you know young ladies should never wear shorts?"

They all laughed and looked relieved, and this time she managed to really laugh with them. "Come on," she said. "Let's go out on the patio till Mom comes home from work with the pizzas. She'll be here soon."

"Speaking of pizzas, those were the greatest invitations I've ever seen," Tricia said. "So great that mine drove Chessie wild," she said of her dog.

"Yeah," Jess said, "delicious smelling. I had to fight my brothers to keep them from eating the pepperonis. Mom says you ought to work for Morelli's. We all got so hungry just smelling it that we ordered pizza from them for dinner!"

"All right!" Becky said, feeling better. "They were fun to make." She'd cut pale yellow posterboard and folded it over to fit into a big manila envelope. On the front of each card, she'd drawn a pizza and glued circles of real microwaved pepperoni on it, then glued wax birthday candles on the dried-out pepperonis. Over the pizza, she'd lettered,

YOU'RE INVITED
TO A
PIZZA BIRTHDAY PARTY

Inside, she'd written,

SLUMBER PARTY TOO!

Next to the date and time, she'd sketched cartoons of each of the girls sleeping, with huge ZZZZZZZZs in the cartoon balloons. She'd drawn Tricia in total collapse behind a stage curtain, clutching a bouquet of flowers; Jess snored on her trampoline; and Cara, who wanted to be a writer, was sound asleep at her desk with pen in hand.

Cara grinned. "Talk about smell-a-cards! Mom said the pepperonis would draw ants, but they haven't yet. I'm going to keep mine forever, even if I have to take the pepperonis off."

Becky remembered leaving the invitations at their doorsteps, ringing the doorbells, and running like everything. "It was fun delivering them," she said. "I thought you'd catch me for sure." Best of all, doing the invitations had kept her mind off her problem.

Outside in their small, fenced yard, their old collie, Lass, looked up from her dog house, then resumed her nap. The

Mexican clay tile patio was already shaded from the late afternoon sun, and the girls settled on the faded cushions of the wooden outdoor furniture. All except Jess, who, as usual, grabbed the nearest patio post and worked on leg stretches, bouncing one foot back, then switching to the other.

A bird chirped from the California pepper tree that sprawled over the fence from Tricia's backyard next door. Everyone looked for the bird in silence. Being quiet together was supposed to be a sign of real friendship, but Becky didn't feel it now. Instead, she felt as if she couldn't pretend much longer.

Tricia lifted her long, reddish-blond hair from her neck as she glanced at the tree. After a while she said about the bird, "Guess we woke him or her."

Becky peered up into the willowy branches, but didn't see it. "Guess so."

They were all looking for the bird in the old pepper tree as if it were terribly important. *They know*, Becky thought. *They know because I'm acting so different*. Worst of all, she couldn't help it.

Jess had one foot against the patio post and her other foot placed firmly on the ground behind her. She put her nose to her knee. "Listen," she told Becky, "we know something's wrong with you. You've been acting weird for a long time, and it's not because of the birthday party. You want to tell us or not?"

Becky tried harder than ever to find the bird in the tree. "Not, I guess."

"Let's not talk about serious stuff now," Tricia said.

Jess shrugged, then started her side stretches. "It's better to get troubles out in the open."

14

"Not always," Cara said. "There's a time for everything, including a time to be quiet. Let's talk about what we're going to do this summer."

Becky only half heard their plans, which they'd already discussed anyhow. In August, Tricia and her family were going to Virginia to visit cousins, and Jess and her family might go to Hawaii. Cara wasn't going anywhere, because her family had bought a video rental store this year. Just hearing their plans again made Becky's feelings roller-coaster.

"What are you doing, Becky?" Jess asked.

She couldn't hold the terrible news another instant. "We're moving!" she blurted. Tears burst to her eyes. "We're moving away!"

"Moving?!" the others repeated in unison.

Becky nodded, angrily wiping away the hot tears. "Yeah, moving. Leaving California! Leaving you . . . and probably never wearing shorts or eating tacos or needing suntan lotion again!"

They stared at her, shocked.

She sniffed. "I didn't want to tell you before."

"Where are you moving to?" Tricia asked.

Becky shook her head. "We don't even know."

"Then why?" Jess asked.

"Because southern California is so expensive . . . and I need braces . . . and we need a new car and a washing machine, and a thousand other reasons. Mom thinks we can sell the house and live much more cheaply in another part of the country. She's got brochures, articles, and books about other states. She's writing to Chambers of Commerce all over the place and even getting some small-town newspapers."

"Oh, Becky!" Tricia wailed. "What will we do without you?"

Becky shrugged. Now she wished she'd kept on pretending until her birthday party was over. Her heart hurt even more now that they knew. For one thing, she and Tricia had lived next door to each other ever since they were babies, and their moms were best friends. For another, she'd miss Jess and Cara awfully, too.

Jess had stopped her side stretches, frowning as she thought. "Maybe you could get a job."

"Like what, baby-sitting?" Becky asked dejectedly. "I can't even baby-sit past ten o'clock."

"Well, you could work later now that school's out," Cara suggested.

Becky shook her head. "It's not enough money to make a difference. The only thing I can think of is maybe trying to sell enough of my greeting cards—you know, hundreds or thousands, instead of only two or three here and there to the neighbors."

"I'd like to work this summer, too," Cara said. "Just for clothes and stuff."

"Me, too," Tricia put in. "But I don't have a humongous money problem like Becky's."

Jess looked hopeful. "If we all put our heads together—"

"And pray about it," Tricia added.

"I've been praying," Becky told them, "but I'm not getting any answers."

"Maybe your mom could get married again," Jess said. "You know, to someone who's rich, like that man she's been dating."

Becky shook her head. "I don't think she wants to. She

still . . . she still loves my father."

No one spoke. They were all no doubt thinking about how sad it would be to have lost their father—killed by a drunk driver no less. It still hurt Becky, even though it had happened two years ago.

The front door banged, and Mrs. Hamilton called out, "Girls! We're home! Happy birthday, Becky!"

Five-year-old Amanda yelled, "Happy birthday, Becky! We brought lots of presents!"

"We're here, Mom," Becky called back, trying to sound as carefree as possible, "out here on the patio."

She warned her friends, "Don't you dare let on that I told you about our moving. And don't tell anyone else, especially not your parents."

"We won't," they promised solemnly.

"Don't forget," Becky warned. "*Please* don't forget."

———

Mom and Amanda sat with them at the birthday table, and, after Mom said grace, everyone began to help themselves to pizza. Amanda's blue eyes darted around at Becky's friends with excitement. She wasn't a bit shy, in spite of her age. "I *love* pizza!" she announced.

"Me, too," Becky agreed, taking a slice with pepperoni. She always felt hungry when she was unhappy. Even though the hot cheese burned her mouth a little, she felt so miserable it didn't even matter. She wasn't going to think about how expensive it was for Mom to have bought pizza from Morelli's, the best pizza parlor in Santa Rosita. She was just going to have a good time.

Amanda put on her important voice. "I helped make your

birthday cake last night, Becky. It's blue and—"

"Remember, we were going to keep it a secret," Mom interrupted, putting a finger to her lips.

Amanda scrunched up her face. "I forgot."

Becky and her friends laughed. Amanda always looked cute, even when she was mischievous. Gram, the girls' grandmother on their mom's side, claimed Amanda looked just like her mother had when she was five: thick dark brown hair, dark eyelashes, big blue eyes, and just plump enough to look cuddly and innocent.

"It's important to keep secrets," Mom told Amanda.

Becky glanced nervously around the table at her friends, and everyone nodded.

"Anyhow," Becky said, "I hope the cake is chocolate." She eyed Amanda, but her sister was busy eating her pizza. Becky took a bite out of her own slice, stringing out the cheese as far as she could.

"Maybe the cake is chocolate," Mom replied, "and maybe it isn't." She had long slender fingers, and she had an elegant way of eating, even pizza. Today, her shoulder-length, dark brown hair was pulled back into a barrette and her blue-green eyes sparkled with fun. Everyone said she was beautiful, and sometimes she modeled on Saturdays for ladies' luncheons. Otherwise, she was busy with her job as an executive secretary at the advertising agency.

"Yeah, maybe the cake is choc'lit and maybe it isn't," Amanda echoed, making the girls hide their smiles.

As they ate, they talked about the last day of school and how hyper everyone had been—and about going into seventh grade! It was fun to sit under the blue crepe paper streamers eating pizza and remembering, and wondering about next year.

For a moment, it felt just like a birthday party should feel. Even the pile of presents on top of the cabinet had grown.

"What are you girls going to do this summer?" Mom asked.

"We're thinking about getting jobs," Jess answered.

Becky panicked, and Tricia quickly put in, "And thinking about resting our brains for a while, too!"

Everyone laughed, and Becky was glad to have the subject changed.

Finally everyone was stuffed with pizza, and Mom and Tricia cleared the table.

"And now for the birthday cake," Mom said, stepping into the kitchen. When she returned to the table, twelve candles blazed over the blue and white cake.

"Happy birthday to you," they all sang out. "You live in the zoo . . ."

"Oh, no!" Becky protested. "Not again!"

She kept her eyes on the flickering candles so she wouldn't get teary and think about moving away.

Then, right while they were singing, a brainstorm hit. They could start a club—the *Twelve Candles Club*—since they were all twelve now, and they could do all sorts of work this summer. Maybe she could even pay her friends to sell her greeting cards, and they could all wash cars and windows . . . maybe even clean houses . . . and, of course, baby-sit. Becky's heart thumped hard. Who knew what all they could do?

Everyone was singing the finale of "Happy Birthday," then chorusing, "And many more!" when she realized that this brainstorm was the answer to her prayers. She'd never in her life been so certain of an answer. If she worked hard enough this summer, they wouldn't have to move. She just knew it.

Mom placed the glowing cake in front of Becky.

"Time to blow out the candles," Tricia said.

"Make a wish," Jess added.

"A good one," Cara put in.

Becky exclaimed, "I've got the answer! It's the Twelve Candles Club!"

They all stared at her strangely, but she closed her eyes and made her wish as if it were a prayer: *Please help us not to have to move.*

Opening her eyes, she blew hard. All twelve flames went out in one big breath.

"The Twelve Candles Club," she said, catching her breath. "That's what we can do!"

CHAPTER

2

What do you mean, a Twelve Candles Club?" chorused Becky's friends.

The smoke from the birthday candles still hung in the air as Becky looked up at them. Mom stared at her, too. But it'd be dumb-dumb-dumb to tell now about making money. "Don't mind me!" she answered a little too fast. "I'm just hyper, with the last day of school and my birthday and everything." It was true, she was hyper. She'd just have to calm down until she could tell them later in her bedroom.

"*Come on*, Becky!" Tricia protested. She looked the most suspicious, having known Becky since their playpen days.

Becky rolled her eyes sideways, warning her to be quiet.

"Oops," Mom said, hopping up from her chair. "Forgot a knife to cut the cake."

The instant she stepped into the kitchen, Becky mouthed to her friends, "A brainstorm. I'll tell you all later."

Their eyes danced with interest, and Amanda demanded, "Tell us what?"

"I'll . . . I'll tell you when you're twelve years old," Becky answered, thinking fast. "It's for twelve-year-olds only. That's why it's called the Twelve Candles Club."

Amanda cocked her head. "You sure?"

"How many pieces of cake do you want?" Becky asked.

"Two," Amanda answered. "Two pieces of cake."

"Then that's what you'll get if you don't ask any more questions," Becky promised.

"Do I hear bribery?" Mom asked, returning to the table. Everyone laughed, and Mom offered, "Want me to cut the birthday cake?"

"Please." Becky, feeling shaky, handed the cake to her mom across the table. She didn't know which excited her more—the birthday cake and presents, or the brainstorm to make money so they wouldn't have to move away.

They all watched as Mom cut into the cake.

"Chocolate!" Becky exclaimed.

Amanda nodded. "I knew it. I wanted choc'lit frosting. But Mama said blue and white frosting to match the blue crepe paper st'eamers."

Becky decided it was no time to correct her little sister's speech. "So you frosted it blue and white so I'd know you weren't color klutzes."

Mom laughed. "Exactly."

When everyone was served, Mom nodded for Becky to take the first bite. It was double chocolately chocolate. In fact, it was so good that even Amanda stopped talking.

Between bites, Becky said, "Can you believe that we used to worry about Amanda-Panda never being able to talk!"

"I'm not Amanda-Panda," her sister announced. "And I can talk!"

"You certainly can," Mom agreed.

They all laughed, except Amanda, who grinned as she forked up another chunk of cake.

As soon as they'd finished and cleared the table, Jess set the presents in front of Becky. "For the birthday girl," Jess announced in her usual take-charge way.

"Wow!" Becky said. "Look at all of these presents."

Amanda pushed one toward her. "Open this one from Gram first. She's sewing a—"

Mom held up a hand, "Let's not spoil the surprise."

Amanda looked indignant. "I was just going to say Gram is sewing one for me just like it, only mine is yellow and white. See, I didn't spoil it!"

The package was wrapped in a blue and white cloth—powder blue with tiny white butterflies—and topped with a matching bow. Gram still worked part-time as an interior decorator, which meant she decorated rooms, but she knew how to make everything else special, too.

Becky opened the card. It had a butterfly on the front of it, with no printing inside. Gram had written in flowing letters,

Have a lovely birthday and a glorious twelfth! Please (you, your mother, and Amanda) save Sunday after church for a birthday brunch at The Beachcomber.

"Keep the wrapping," Amanda ordered. "It's to wear."

"Looks like a stole," Becky guessed, unsure if she'd actually wear it. She opened the package and pulled out a blue and white dress of the same fabric. It had narrow shoulder straps and a drop waist, with a flared skirt. She took a closer look at the stole. It wasn't old-fashioned at all. In fact, it could be attached to the dress to cover her shoulders. "It's beautiful!"

"Here's another present from Gram," Amanda said.

This one was wrapped in light blue paper with eyelet lace trim, and a big red paper heart in the middle. Inside was a cloth doll wearing a blue and white butterfly dress to match her own.

"She's a dec'ration for your bed," Amanda said.

Becky admired the doll. "Isn't she cute? I'm going to call her Jeannie—for Gram."

"Gram's something else, isn't she?" Mom said.

Becky nodded. "She sure is!"

"Now my present," Amanda insisted. She handed over a small package and a homemade blue card covered with candles. Gram baby-sat Amanda most afternoons after her morning preschool. She must have shown her how to write the words, but the

HAPPY BIRTHDAY, BECKY

greeting was crooked.

"Nice," Becky said, then tore into the package. Inside was a blue hair bow to match the sundress.

"Gram helped me buy it," Amanda said. "It's for your hair orn'ment collection."

"Thanks," Becky said. "If there's one thing I like, it's hair *orn'ments!*"

Everyone smiled, including Amanda.

Becky reached for the next present. It was from Jess—a beautiful Hawaiian white coral necklace.

Next came Cara's white package with the huge blue Mexican crepe paper flower. Inside, she found a jumbo sketch pad. "Wow, just what I needed!" Becky said, then removed the white tissue paper from something else wrapped with it. A videotape, which wasn't surprising since Cara's parents owned a video store. She turned the tape over in her hand. "There's no label—"

"It's a surprise," Cara said, her big brown eyes shining. "You'll know what it is when we see it."

"Hmmm . . . a mystery present," Becky said. "Thanks, I love mysteries."

Cara smiled, looking hopeful.

Becky opened the other presents. A set of colored pencils and a denim skirt from Mom; a $25 check from her grandparents in Indiana; and a blue, white, and green T-shirt from Tricia.

"Blue and green because they're both of our favorite colors," Tricia explained.

"What awesome presents!" Becky said and thanked each of them again as they got up from the table.

"Let's see the mystery tape," Tricia suggested.

Becky drew a deep breath. Eager as she was to see it, she was dying to tell them about the Twelve Candles Club. But she'd be polite and show Cara's video first. "Come on." She grabbed the tape and headed for the living room.

It was a small living room, their house being the smallest model in the Santa Rosita Estates. She opened the doors of the bleached white armoire, where they kept the TV and VCR, and stuck in Cara's video.

"I wanna see it, too!" Amanda said.

Mom turned Amanda around gently. "It's Becky's slumber

25

party now, so we'll stay out of the way. After we clean up the kitchen, I'll read to you in my bedroom."

Becky heaved a sigh of relief. She loved her sister, but enough was enough. She grabbed the remote control and plopped down on the floor in front of the couch with her friends. "Ready?"

"Ready!" they answered.

Cara hid a smile behind her hand, making Becky suspicious.

The tape began, and suddenly they were all there on the screen. Everything looked familiar, but Becky racked her brain to remember where they were.

"It's Cara's tenth birthday party!" Tricia exclaimed. "All right! Whoa, didn't we look . . . crazy?!"

On the screen, they were all jumping up and down, clowning around in Cara's family room. Becky gave a laugh. "I forgot you took these pictures! Oh . . . look, it's Jess trying to show us how to turn cartwheels! Oh, no, look at me!"

Everyone roared with laughter. As usual, Becky was too tall and lanky to turn one, and she looked like a number-one klutz, not that Tricia or Cara were much better at cartwheels. Just as funny were Jess's exasperated looks as she watched them fling themselves through the air. "You klutzes!" she'd yelled. Funniest of all, they were all laughing like mad on the videotape too.

From the family room at Cara's house, the video showed them moving into the kitchen, where they balanced pots and pans on their heads, and Tricia spoke with great drama into a small sieve,

Oh, a wonderful horse is the Fly-Away Horse—

Perhaps you have seen him before;
Perhaps, while you slept, his shadow has swept
Through the moonlight that floats on the floor . . .

She would have recited the entire "Fly-Away Horse" if Jess hadn't yanked the sieve-microphone from her.

"Approaching planet Mars," Jess said into the sieve. "Final approach to planet Mars."

Then it was out to the garage, where they got into Cara's mom's van and pretended to be driving to the grand opening of Tricia's first Hollywood movie.

"I can't believe we did that!" Becky said. Her jaws hurt from laughing. "Look at Tricia being the actress! Just look at her chin sticking up in the air. And Jess pretending to be carsick. Gross! I can't believe it!"

They laughed harder, holding their stomachs.

Next, on a dare, they'd run outside around the house in their pajamas . . . Becky in her old Minnie Mouse sleepshirt, too! After that, they'd sneaked into the kitchen to eat the rest of Cara's birthday cake.

"Oh, I hurt from laughing," Becky said, and everyone else did, too. "I can't believe this . . ."

Finally, there were close-ups of them sound asleep in their sleeping bags the next morning.

"Who took these?" Becky asked.

Cara laughed. "Mom did. She thought it'd be the perfect ending for a slumber party."

"What a super present," Becky said as she rewound the tape. "We might have acted dumb, but I'm glad we can always remember. Especially if I . . ." She stopped in time. She'd almost said, *Especially if I move away.*

They must have known what she meant, though, because they all stopped laughing.

"Come on," she told them. "Let's go to my room."

———

In her room, Becky settled her new Jeannie doll among the throw pillows. "She looks perfect," Becky decided.

"Just like your room," Cara said. "It's like one of those rooms in your Gram's decorating magazines. Wish we had a decorator in my family," she added wistfully.

Her small bedroom did look nice, Becky thought. It had blue carpet and lots of blue, white, and yellow accents. Gram called the beds "a corner group unit with drawers." They were really just white bunk beds, and the head of one slid under the other. Below each one were blue drawers for socks and undies and folded stuff.

Gram had bought powder-blue comforters and sewn big yellow and white daisies on them, then made coordinated pillows with huge daisies and white eyelet edging. She'd also stenciled matching daisies here and there on the white walls. A white desk surrounded by bookshelves stood across the room. And behind the door was a full-length mirror with daisies stenciled around it.

"Let's pull out the bottom bunk farther, so we can all sit on the beds," Becky said.

Tricia helped, since she was used to pulling the lower bunk out from having already slept there a thousand times.

Becky climbed up on her bunk and Tricia clambered up beside her. "Okay, so what's with this Twelve Candles Club brainstorm?"

Becky drew an excited breath. "Remember, out on the

patio we talked about making money this summer?"

"Sure, we remember." Jess nodded, plopping down next to Cara on the lower bunk.

"Well, I prayed and wished like anything before blowing out the birthday candles, and it just came to me. The Twelve Candles Club—since we're all twelve years old!"

"I don't get it," Tricia said.

"I thought we could get jobs together," Becky explained. "And we'd need a name for a working club. The Twelve Candles Club—that's what we could call it. It'd be lots more fun to work together. You all said you'd like to work this summer, right?"

"You mean work together like helpers at kids' birthday parties and stuff?" Tricia asked.

Becky brightened. "I hadn't thought of that, but it's a good idea. Maybe we could help at grown-up parties, too."

"Hey! We could be a baby-sitting team and have the kids do skits," Tricia said. "I can get skit books from the library."

"Maybe skits with some gymnastics," Jess said. "Wow! We could do all kinds of fun things. You know, like have a preschool, with crafts and field trips, too. No babies, though. They wouldn't fit in. Around Amanda's age and a little older."

Becky beamed. "How about ages four to seven? I'm going to have to baby-sit Amanda a lot anyhow this summer, so that would be perfect."

"And I'm going to have to baby-sit Bryan and Suzanne a lot, too," Tricia said of her five-year-old brother and seven-year-old sister. "We could have it at my house, since we have swings and stuff. I'll bet Mom wouldn't mind, and she'll be home too. Should I call her now?"

Everyone agreed and, minutes later, when Tricia returned

29

from the kitchen phone, she bounced with excitement. "We're on! Mom thinks it's a great idea. She'll even help if we need it."

"You know, I was thinking of more practical jobs, too," Becky said, "like washing cars and windows, and maybe housecleaning. You know, dusting and vacuuming."

Tricia bounced on the bed. "We could do *all of it*! Oh, Becky, I'd do almost anything so you wouldn't have to move!"

Jess and Cara agreed, and Becky had to blink hard, realizing how much they cared. "But I couldn't take your money. I couldn't. I'd only want my share."

"Then we'd have to make lots of money together and somehow split it up," Cara said.

"Maybe we could help sell your pizza cards," Jess suggested. "You could pay us a fee like what my mom gets for selling houses. You know what she said about those pizza cards making people hungry! We could start tomorrow at Morelli's Pizza Parlor. I'll give you back my card so you could show them what they're like."

"I don't know," Becky said. "It's easy to sell cards to neighbors and Mom's friends, but I don't know about going out to sell them."

"Now's no time to hold back," Jess argued. "If you want to make money, you're going to have to try new things."

"I guess so."

"What else?" Tricia asked. "Let's think."

"Well, we could help sell the birthday cards you've made, too," Cara said. "But I think you should sell the pizza cards to Morelli's yourself."

"Right," Tricia agreed.

Jess sat with the bottoms of her feet together, bouncing her legs. "There's another thing. The *Santa Rosita Times* is giving free ads for kids' summer jobs this week. They allow one short line. You know, like *Yardwork, Window washing*, and a phone number. At least that's what my brothers wrote."

"We could hand out fliers, too," Cara said. "Maybe my parents would give them out at the video store."

"What about baby-sitting?" Tricia asked. "We've all done some."

"But we'd have to baby-sit by ourselves, and we want to do things together," Cara answered.

"Well, let's write it down," Tricia said. "We can always turn jobs down if we want to."

Becky climbed down from the bunk and headed for her desk. "Let's make a list or we'll forget half of it." She grabbed a pencil and a pad of paper. "Okay. Tell me again."

As they talked, she wrote:

JOBS
party helpers
sell cards
kids' morning fun school (4–7 years old)
washing cars and windows
dusting and vacuuming houses
baby-sitting

HOW TO GET THEM
ads in Santa Rosita Times
fliers to hand out
take sample pizza card to Morelli's
make sample greeting cards

"Let's write the ads now," Jess said. "They're due at the

newspaper tomorrow. Mom's taking my brothers' ads in. She could take ours, too."

"What should we say?" Becky asked. "There's too much to put in one line."

Cara raised her chin, thoughtful. "How about *Four girl workers*? Each of us will list the same ad, but with our own phone number. That way we could get four free ads. What do you think?"

"Sounds good to me," Jess said.

"What will we say when people call?" Becky asked.

Jess thought a moment. "We can say, 'May I call you back after our meeting?' And, if that's not soon enough, we'll have to call each other and decide what to do. We'll have to figure it out as we go."

"Now the fliers," Tricia suggested. "There're thirty or forty houses on our street, and we could give out fliers all around the neighborhood. Put them in mailboxes. We'll need at least a hundred. Maybe even two hundred."

Becky tore off another piece of paper. "They'd charge us a lot at the photocopy place."

Jess gave her knees a good bounce. "No problem! We have a copy machine at home in Dad's office. I'm sure he'll let us do them for free."

"Great. Well, then, what'll we write?" Cara asked. "What's on your notes, Becky?"

Becky read the list aloud, then frowned. "We've got to make it sound better."

Five pieces of paper later, she lettered their final version.

TWELVE CANDLES CLUB
   Four 12-year-old girls will do all kinds of jobs for you this

summer. Here are a few of them:
— Party Helpers
— Morning Fun for Kids (ages 4–7) M-W-F 9–12 a.m.
   (skits, games, crafts, neighborhood outings)
   5525 La Crescenta Way,
   Santa Rosita Estates
— Car & Window washing
— Dusting & Vacuuming
—˙Baby-sitting until 10 p.m.
— Custom Greeting Cards & Invitations

"We ought to have one phone number or it's going to be a mess," Cara suggested. "In case we get a lot of calls, it'd be best to have someone with their own phone."

They all turned to Jess, who grinned. "Why not?"

"Just one phone number?" Tricia asked. "Why not give all of our numbers like in the newspaper ads?"

"Because we're doing that to get *four* free ads. For the fliers, one phone number is best," Cara said.

"I guess so," Tricia said, giving in.

"Besides," Jess added, "if we have meetings at my house, I can work out on my equipment while we talk. But if we're going to spend so much time working, we'll need a special time for phone calls."

"Just before dinner every night except weekends," Tricia suggested. "Four-thirty to five-thirty, so we can still set the table at home and stuff."

Cara looked at Jess. "Will you be home from gymnastics then?"

Jess nodded, and when everyone had agreed, Becky wrote Jess's personal phone number and the times on the bottom of the page.

They all eyed the flier.

"Too plain," Tricia said. "It needs some of your famous artwork, Becky."

"I've got it!" she said. She sketched in twelve flaming candles while her friends stood around her and watched. "What do you think?"

"Lots better," Tricia decided, "but still a little empty. Maybe you could sketch us in, sort of like those cartoons you did on the pizza invitations. But only our faces."

"It's not easy to draw faces," Becky said hesitantly.

"Try it," Cara put in. "They don't have to be so good or in living color, only smiling."

"If you think so." Becky looked at each of them, then sketched. *Tricia:* an oval face with thick eyebrows and long, slightly wavy hair. *Jess:* a square face with a strong chin and her dark blond hair cut short. *Cara:* a heart-shaped face with big eyes and long, thick, wavy black hair. *Herself:* an oval face with a lips-turned-up smile and long brown hair held back by a headband.

"We look friendly," Cara said. "It's really good."

"Yes!" Tricia raised her hands to lead a cheer for the Twelve Candles Club. "Let's hear it for the Twelve Candles Club!"

"All right!" they cheered. "Yea for the Twelve Candles Club!"

"Yea!" Becky cheered again with them, hoping like everything that it would really work.

CHAPTER

3

The next morning, Becky awoke before her friends. After a while, she heard Mom getting Amanda up for preschool, which didn't let out for two more days.

Becky quietly climbed down from her bunk, grabbed the Twelve Candles Club flier, and tiptoed between her sleeping friends. Closing the door carefully, she padded down the hallway in her summer nightshirt toward the kitchen.

"Up already?" her mom asked. Her dark hair was pulled back in a barrette again, and she wore a beige suit and high heels. Like it or not, she looked like a career woman, even though she'd only been a secretary at the advertising agency since Dad died. She smiled. "With all that laughing and cheering, I thought you'd sleep till noon."

"Did we keep you up?"

"Not *too* late," Mom said with a smile as she whizzed around the kitchen. "I've put breakfast on the table—cereal, rolls, bran muffins. There's orange juice in the refrigerator and plenty of milk."

"Thanks for a fun birthday party, Mom."

"My pleasure," she answered, planting a kiss on the top of Becky's head. "What's the paper?"

"We'd like to start a working club this summer. Here, see what you think. Jess says she can make copies of it at home for a handout in the neighborhood."

Mom scanned the flier, raising her eyebrows. "Why, Rebecca Anne Hamilton, I'm impressed. But it looks like a lot of work. Can you handle that much responsibility?"

Becky swallowed. They'd talked about the fun and the money, but nothing else. "I think so. If the jobs are too hard or something, we'll turn them down."

"Where would you have the Morning Fun for Kids?" Mom asked.

"At Tricia's. Her mom already agreed, and even said she'd be there if we need help."

Becky's mother raised her dark brows again. "Well, then, it sounds like good experience for all of you."

"I thought maybe we could use my $25 check from Nana and Gramp Hamilton to help pay household bills."

Her mother shook her head. "I appreciate your offer, Becky, but I was really hoping you'd use it for new white sandals, and to help replace your tennies. You're outgrowing your shoes. Besides, your tennies are holey—and I don't mean *holy*. I mean disreputable." She glanced at her watch just as Amanda appeared in the doorway, looking half-asleep. "We've gotta hurry! Phone me at work so I know where you'll be." With that, she and Amanda were out the door and on their way to work and preschool.

When Becky opened her bedroom door, her friends were just beginning to wake up and stretch in their sleeping bags. "Morning, sleepyheads. Guess what? Mom thinks the Twelve Candles Club is a great idea!"

"I hope my father will, too," Cara said, doubt in her voice. "You know how strict he can be sometimes."

"He might be strict, but he's the most handsome father around," Becky said. The others nodded their agreement.

At breakfast, they began to make their plans.

Jess, who lived ten houses south of Becky on the same street, would take the advertisements for the *Santa Rosita Times* to her mother, and get the handouts copied. Cara, who lived across from Jess, had to catch her father before he left for work and ask for permission for everything. Tricia would take her stuff home, then bike down to the library for books on crafts and skits for little kids. And Becky would make a new pizza party invitation, without the sketches of the girls inside, so that Mr. Morelli would know exactly what the crazy invitations were like.

At nine o'clock they were all on their way, and at ten-thirty the girls returned with their bikes.

"Ready, Becky?" they yelled through the screened kitchen window. "We all got permission, even Cara!"

Becky ran to open the front door. "I just have to cover the pizza card with plastic so the envelope doesn't get greasy."

The girls all trooped into the house.

Jess eyed the breakfast leftovers on the kitchen counter. "Maybe we'd better take the rolls and muffins in case we get hungry. I brought some bananas, the only fruit my brothers hadn't scarfed down. I also brought a big bag of corn chips."

Becky put the breakfast rolls and muffins in plastic bags. "I phoned Mom, and she said we could take granola bars and packs of apple juice." She gathered everything together and put them in her blue backpack. "We won't make much profit if we have to buy lunches," she said, zipping it up. "Ready!"

She wore white shorts and her new blue and green T-shirt from Tricia, who wore one just like it. "Mom thought it'd be fun for us to have matching T-shirts," Tricia said.

"It sure is," Becky agreed, pleased to be dressed like her best friend.

Outside, Jess showed them the stack of handouts she'd copied. "They really look good. Maybe we should pay you for them," Becky said.

"No, Dad's investing in our cause," Jess answered. "He says any money I make will be a savings to him."

"Way to go, Mr. McColl!" Becky cheered. She slipped the manila envelope with the pizza party invitation under her bike rack, then hopped onto the seat and pedaled out to the street with her friends. It was a bright, sunny day, and suddenly Becky yelled, "Hey, it really feels like summer vacation has begun!"

"It does!" Jess agreed. She led the way as they rode along in the bike lane toward Ocean Avenue. Morelli's Pizza Parlor was located in a small shopping strip near Flicks—Cara's father's video place—and only two miles away.

It was mostly downhill riding toward the ocean. Pedaling along, Becky tried to figure out what to say. *Ah . . . Mr. Morelli, I had this idea . . . this WONDERFUL idea to sell a lot of pizzas.*

He'll probably say, "We already sell lots of pizzas!"

Yes, Mr. Morelli, we had pizza at my birthday party last night, and we liked it so much, we thought others would—

Phooey! Mr. Morelli will think the whole thing is a dumb kids' idea and throw us out. In fact, the closer they rode to Ocean Avenue, the dumber the idea seemed to Becky.

As they passed the *Santa Rosita Times* building, Becky yelled back to Cara, "Wonder if we'll get any phone calls from the ads?"

"I hope so," Cara answered.

Finally, they crossed Ocean Avenue and pedaled into the shopping area parking. Morelli's Pizza Parlor loomed ahead, a brown wooden building with Christmas lights edging the roof and windows. It stood by itself near the street, away from the rest of the shops.

Jess rode straight to the bike racks.

"Scared?" Tricia asked as they pulled up.

Becky nodded. "The whole idea seems crazy."

Tricia put on her Cheshire cat smile. "All the better."

Jess locked up her bike and grabbed the folder with the handouts. "Cara and I are going to Flicks to see if her father will pass out these fliers to his customers. It's best if only two go into Morelli's, rather than all of us."

"You chickens!" Tricia accused as they locked their bikes.

Jess and Cara laughed, and ran like everything toward the video store.

Becky knew how they felt. She pulled the manila envelope from under her bike rack. "At least it's not greasy from the pepperonis. Come on."

Tricia fell into step with her. "You can do it, Becky. I'll stand behind you and pray real hard."

Becky clapped her fingers to her lips. "I forgot all about praying! Let's stop a minute."

Standing by the newspaper racks in front of Morelli's, Becky prayed, *Lord, forgive me for being so busy with my birthday and slumber party, and the Twelve Candles Club, that I almost forgot about you. I don't know if Mr. Morelli will want these dumb invitations or not, but I pray that your will be done in all of this, even—even if we do have to move away. In Jesus' powerful name, I pray. Amen.*

When Becky looked up, she saw that Tricia was praying, too. It was probably easier for Tricia because her grandfather was a minister, and she was used to it. It was different for Becky and her mom, who hadn't really become Christians until just before Dad died two years ago. She and Tricia were the only believers in the club, she guessed. At least Cara and Jess didn't go to church or talk much about God.

The instant Tricia opened her eyes, Becky said, "Let's go before I get chicken myself!" She took the pizza invitation out of the envelope and removed the plastic wrap. "You carry this junk, Trish. It'll look better if I just carry in the card. Thank goodness the glue is still holding the pepperonis and candles in place."

Tricia grabbed the envelope and plastic, then held Morelli's front door open for Becky. "You're in charge."

Becky walked in, swallowing once, then again. She whispered, "I should have rehearsed." Why didn't she ever think before she acted?

A high school boy came to the cash register. "May I help you?"

Becky stammered, "I—I'd like to see Mr. Morelli, please."

"And what about, may I ask?" he inquired.

"Business," she answered, her voice firmer.

He eyed her suspiciously, then headed for the kitchen.

"You think he'll get him?" Becky asked Tricia. "Or does he just think we're dumb kids?"

Tricia's green eyes widened. "Here comes Mr. Morelli now. You're on, Beck. You're on!"

Mr. Morelli was a short, dark man with graying hair, who wore a white chef's hat and apron. "Well, ladies," he boomed, "what can I do for you this fine morning?"

Becky cleared her throat. "I . . . I make these pizza party invitations, and I thought you might want to set one out for people to order."

"Show him the card, Becky," Tricia hissed.

Heat rushed to Becky's face as she turned the card around so he could see it. "If . . . if customers order the cards from me, I thought they'd buy your pizza for their parties."

Mr. Morelli took the big invitation from Becky and looked it over. "Well, what an idea! A picture of a pizza with real pepperonis and real candles! This must be the one that brought Mrs. McColl rushing in here the other night. She told me about it."

Becky nodded. "That's my friend Jess's mother."

Mr. Morelli smiled at her. "I think we could get lots of orders for you. And then we'd get more orders for pizza here! Looks like you have a big investment in it too: poster board, candles, real pepperoni." He opened it to read the inside:

Place:

Date:

Time:

Available with or without birthday candles. Envelopes included. Call 590–2717.

"How much you want for one of these?" he asked.

Becky hesitated. "I thought $2.00, or maybe $2.50, depending on what you charge to sell them for me."

Mr. Morelli smiled. "You can get $2.50 easy. People pay that much for birthday cards nowadays anyway, and this is something special. I'll set your card up here on the counter over the cheesecakes, and as soon as I get an order I'll call you."

"You'll call me?"

"Sure! Straight and simple. No fuss," Mr. Morelli smiled again. "I display your invitation, and take orders for you at no charge—and the customers buy more of my pizza!"

"At no charge?"

He nodded. "No charge. I like to see smart kids get ahead."

"Thanks, Mr. Morelli! That's even better than I expected!"

He reached out to shake Becky's hand. "Partners," he said. "Partners in the pizza business. You make any other invitations?"

"I guess I could make any kind people want. I make greeting cards, too."

"Bring 'em along next time. Can't say I'd sell 'em here, but I might buy some myself." He gave a loud laugh. "Especially pizza birthday cards! Wouldn't that be something? We got lots of birthdays in my family."

"Thanks," Becky said again. She had a feeling it was time to leave, and she backed out. "Thanks again!" She backed up faster and stumbled onto Tricia's foot.

"Ouch!" Tricia yelled, then slapped a hand over her mouth.

"Oh, Trish, I'm sorry!"

Tricia grabbed Becky by the elbow to catch her balance, and Becky stomped on her other foot. "Oh, no, I'm sorry!"

Not only was she acting like the world's number-one klutz, but right here in Morelli's!

Finally, she helped Tricia hop toward the door. Glancing back, she saw her pizza invitation displayed on the countertop, and Mr. Morelli shaking with laughter as he retreated to the kitchen.

By the time they got to their bikes, Becky had apologized twenty times, and Tricia was walking on her own again. "I can't believe he wants to sell my invitations! I just can't believe it!"

"That's what Gramp says happens when you pray," Tricia said. "A lot of I-can't-believe-its. Even more than watching that crazy birthday video last night."

"You know, everything was just about perfect," Becky said, "except for my not showing the invitation to Mr. Morelli right away, and backing out so fast that I almost trampled you to death. I'm sorry, Trish, are you really all right?"

"I may live," she answered, stifling a giggle. "You should have seen yourself backing up on me, Becky. You looked wacko—a backo wacko!" She began to laugh harder, until she doubled over. "I had no idea you could back up so fast! From now on, when you're trying to sell something, I'm not going to stand right behind you. You're downright dangerous!"

They'd just started to head for Flicks when Cara and Jess walked out the door. They didn't look nearly as excited as Becky felt. "What's wrong?"

Cara shook her head. "My father won't give the handouts to strangers, only to people he knows. He says we should be careful in the neighborhood too, because of weirdos."

"I guess he's right," Becky answered. "I was so excited about the whole idea, I didn't think about any danger."

"When we get phone calls from our newspaper ads," Jess said, "we'll have to find out if the people are okay. Mr. Hernandez says we should give them references on ourselves—you know, someone who'll say we're reliable and all. Then it won't be so embarrassing to ask for references from them."

Everyone was silent for a few moments, then Tricia said, "Decent people will understand. That's what my grandfather always says, anyhow."

"I hope so," Becky answered. "Maybe we could give each other's parents for references. They've all known us for a long time." She pulled her bicycle from the rack and hopped on it. "Let's go eat lunch at Seaview Park. Then we can decide what to do next."

They pedaled down Ocean Avenue for another block, then turned right on Seaview Boulevard to the grassy park. It wasn't a big park, but it was great for sitting under the trees at picnic benches and eating lunch. Best of all, you could look out at the ocean in the distance.

As they rode into Seaview Park, Becky thought about Paul Bradshaw, the man who dated Mom. He lived on Seaview Boulevard in one of the houses overlooking the ocean. She'd been cool to him, but maybe he had some car-washing or window-washing work they could do this afternoon.

"Let's get that last picnic bench," Jess said. Even though no one else was near it, she pedaled fast toward it.

Becky followed on her bike, noticing that mothers and their children sat at most of the other picnic tables. "Look, the kids here seem about the right age for Morning Fun for Kids. Maybe we could give fliers to their moms."

"Let's eat first," Cara said as they got off their bikes. "Then it won't look like we came here to pounce on them."

"Come on, now's our chance!" Jess argued. "They probably all live around here and can afford the Morning Fun classes, and everything else. Tricia, you're our best speaker. You tell them about it, and I'll hand out the fliers."

Tricia rolled her eyes at Becky, looking like she wished they'd rehearsed this, too. "Okay," Tricia said. "Just make sure you all act friendly and grown-up."

At the closest picnic table, she told their names. In her best grown-up voice, she said, "We're members of the Twelve Candles Club. That means we're all twelve-years-old, and looking for jobs this summer. We're experienced at all kinds of work. Jess, here, will give you our flier."

Jess handed out the fliers, her lips frozen into a smile.

While the mothers scanned the handouts, Tricia told the smaller kids, "You look just the right age for our Morning Fun for Kids program. We're going to have skits, crafts, games— all kinds of fun. It's on Mondays, Wednesdays, and Fridays, and we live over in Santa Rosita Estates."

One of the mothers asked, "Can the children come one or two days a week, instead of all three?"

"As many as you want," Tricia answered confidently.

"How about snacks?" another mother asked.

They'd forgotten about snacks! Becky said the first things that flew to mind: "We'll have packs of raisins, graham crackers, and apple juice." Despite Tricia's strange look, Becky didn't back down.

"How much does a morning cost?" the first mother asked. They hadn't decided for sure, but Jess blurted out, "Six dollars per child." She rushed on, "It's less than most baby-sitters charge for three hours, and the kids would have fun."

"And learn crafts," Cara put in.

"And skits," Tricia added.

Finally, the mothers looked satisfied.

"See you there, we hope!" Becky said, not able to think of anything else.

"Have a good picnic," Tricia added.

As they left, Becky told Tricia, "Please notice that this time I didn't step on your foot."

"Only because I wasn't behind you," Tricia laughed. "How did I sound?"

"Not rehearsed," Becky said.

"You mean bad?"

"I mean . . . very good, as usual."

Tricia laughed and elbowed her in the ribs.

Jess led the way to the next table, getting out the fliers. "Tricia, you do the talking again. I only wish we could do something they'd remember us by."

Tricia introduced them again. As she told about Morning Fun for Kids, Jess gave the fliers to Cara to hand out, then suddenly turned a backflip.

"Wow!" the little kids yelled as Jess turned another. "Wow, look at that!"

Jess positioned herself to stand on her hands and flipped up. Walking on her hands, she grinned while she talked to them.

"Would you teach us how to do that?" one of the kids asked.

Jess continued walking on her hands. "If your mother says I can," she answered. "Guess we'd need it in writing. My mom always says you can't have too much in writing." Because her mother was a realtor, Jess knew things like that.

At the last two picnic tables, they did the very same routine, with Jess cartwheeling all over and walking on her hands again. The kids and their mothers were as delighted as if a clown had come to perform free of charge.

When they returned to their own picnic table, Jess asked, "How did we do?"

"Great!" Cara said. "I'll bet some will come."

As they settled down to eat, Becky pulled off her backpack and took out the food. Three rolls, four bran muffins, corn chips, bananas, granola bars, and four apple juice boxes didn't look like much in the middle of the picnic table, but it would do.

"Guess we should have made sandwiches," Cara said.

Jess grabbed a bran muffin. "We can eat sandwiches at home. Besides, we have more important things to do. Where else can we hand out the fliers?"

Becky hesitated. "I was thinking about Paul Bradshaw. *Mister* Bradshaw. You know, the one Mom dates sometimes. He lives right here on Seaview Boulevard. What do you think?"

"The one with the handsome sons?" Tricia asked.

"I guess they are," Becky answered. "I only went out to dinner with all of them that one time, and we didn't talk much. We had to drive them back here first because they had to get to a basketball game. Their mother died of cancer last year."

"That's too bad," Cara said.

Tricia began bouncing around on the bench while she ate, a sure sign she was eager. "I think we should start there."

Becky still felt uneasy, then thought about having to move away. "Okay. We can start there."

When they'd finished their lunch, they stuffed the trash into the garbage container and climbed on their bikes. "You know," Cara said, "we were so busy we didn't even look out at the ocean."

Becky turned to look. In the distance, the blue water sparkled in the sunlight. Waves rushed toward the beach, washing ashore and leaving foamy edges on the sand. "I hope we won't be so busy working that we can't go to the beach much this summer."

"We can go every Sunday after church," Tricia said. "You and I can't work on Sundays, anyhow."

Becky waited for Jess or Cara to say something, and Jess finally said, "We need at least one day off a week. And don't forget, I have afternoon gymnastics on the same days we have Morning Fun for Kids."

Moments later, they were pedaling their bikes down Seaview Boulevard. It really was a boulevard, with big pine trees and petunias in the street divider. And it wasn't a newer development like Santa Rosita Estates, where the houses were close together. Here, a few houses were ultra-modern, but most were old Spanish style with red-tiled roofs. Becky glanced through the pine trees and recognized the Bradshaw house. "There it is." So far, it was the only weathered gray shake house with a front porch.

Cara pedaled her bike alongside Becky. "Think he's home?"

Becky nodded. "He's mostly retired. But sometimes he has to fly around the country to help people. He's a—oh, what do you call it? A consultant!" She yelled ahead to Jess and Tricia, "Hang a left here!"

They rode through an opening in the petunias and pine trees to the other side of the boulevard. "It's a really nice house," Cara remarked. "Not flashy or flamboyant like some expensive houses are."

Becky nodded. "Mom says there's nothing flamboyant about Paul Bradshaw; he's just a nice person. In fact, he goes to our church. That's where Mom met him, then he came out jogging with Mr. Keegan on our street."

"Oh, really?" Cara asked.

It sounded fishy, all right, Becky thought. What she suspected was that he jogged on their street on Saturday mornings just to see Mom. He seemed to like her a lot.

They rode up the concrete driveway, and Mr. Bradshaw must have been sitting on the porch, because he came down the steps right away. "Becky!" he exclaimed with a big smile. "What a nice surprise!"

He looked nice himself with his short blond-gray hair, beard and mustache. He wore a yellow and blue sport shirt with a white collar, and white pants and shoes. Becky guessed he liked blue and yellow, like she did, which helped her feel better.

"We're handing out fliers about our working club," she said. They all stood astride their bikes, and she introduced Jess, Cara, and Tricia.

Jess got out the fliers, and Becky gave one to him. "This tells what we do. Anybody who hires us has to have references, though." She stopped, wishing she hadn't sounded so abrupt.

"Good idea," he answered. He took the handout, raising his eyebrows as he read. "Hmmm. You ought to find plenty of work with so many options. In fact, I wouldn't be surprised if you couldn't work right away for Mrs. Llewellyn next door. Actually, it's amazing. She phoned half an hour or so ago to ask if I knew of a cleaning woman, and one who helps with parties. She's having a big barbecue tomorrow, and her cleaning woman is sick. Why don't you come in, and I'll give her a call?"

They parked their bikes in the driveway and followed Mr. Bradshaw up the walk. Suddenly a wild idea flew to Becky's mind: *What if Jess decides to do a back flip and walk on her hands for him like she did for the kids at the park?* It was all she could do not to laugh out loud. Why did such wacko ideas come to her mind at just the wrong moment? *Stop it!* she told herself, and tried to concentrate on walking up the porch steps with Mr. Bradshaw.

He held the front door open for them, but Becky hesitated. "Maybe we'd better . . . that is, it would be fine to wait on your porch." He wasn't exactly a stranger, but Becky didn't feel she knew him well enough to go into his house.

"Make yourself at home," he said. "Try out the porch swing if you like."

Becky guessed he must have been reading the morning paper when they came, because it lay on the swing. She put it down on the floor and settled on the swing beside Jess.

As they pushed off, Jess whispered, "He's a little old for your mother, but he's really nice. Mom says houses in this neighborhood are worth a fortune, and this one is big."

"He's only a friend, so relax," she whispered back. "Mom isn't interested in getting married, and I don't want a new father. I already have a perfectly good father in heaven."

After that, they were all quiet until Tricia said, "I wonder where his sons are."

At last, Mr. Bradshaw returned to the porch. "Mrs. Llewellyn can't wait to meet you. She'd like you to come right over. You can probably work a few hours today. She's somewhat eccentric, but she's nice. I'd be glad to act as her reference."

"Wow, thanks!" Becky said, jumping to her feet. "I don't know how I can thank you enough!"

He smiled. "Glad to help."

The rest of them looked as pleased and excited as Becky felt. She just hoped that Mrs. Llewellyn wouldn't be *too* eccentric—whatever that meant.

CHAPTER

4

*N*ext door, Mrs. Llewellyn's ultra-modern white stucco house rose two stories high in front and three stories from the downward-sloping backyard. It was impressive. Becky and the others rode their bikes over, parking them on the curved driveway by the front door. "Wonder what he means by *eccentric*?" Becky asked.

"Dramatic, maybe," Tricia said. "We'll see."

As they headed for the huge double-door entry, Becky felt like giggling. "Looks like a butler from one of those old movies could open the door."

Jess pressed the doorbell. "Wouldn't that be something!"

They could hear the doorbell pealing out grandiose notes inside the house.

Instead of a butler, however, an elderly woman with frazzled red hair came to the door. The cocker spaniel bustling at her feet was a pale reddish color, too. "You must be the girls

Paul Bradshaw sent over!" the woman said in an excited, squawky voice. "I'm Mrs. Llewellyn. Come in, girls, come in! You can't imagine what a godsend you are."

She scrutinized each of them through thick glasses that magnified her green eyes. "This way, please, girls." She hurried along, stifflegged as a bird. "We'll start in the kitchen and pantry. You girls couldn't have come at a better time! Now, this sweet cocker is called Lulu—short for Llewellyn. I'll keep her out from underfoot."

Flapping her hands as she spoke, Mrs. Llewellyn led the girls and Lulu through the grand hallway entrance flanked with huge plants and modern-type sculptures. "The phone's been ringing off the hook," she complained, although she sounded pleased too. "I don't know how anyone can expect me to have a party if they're forever phoning."

The huge white kitchen had a clay tile floor, stainless steel counters, and copper pots and pans hanging from the high ceiling. The phone rang again, and Mrs. Llewellyn took it off the hook and pressed the button to disconnect it.

"They'll call again if it's important." She laughed, then let Lulu out the kitchen door. "Now, girls, here's the silver polish. I'll need you to polish all the silver pieces and flatware, and wash the crystal and china, too. Oh, and the vases. We'll need vases for lots of fresh flowers. No breakage, mind you." She peered at the girls over her glasses. "And all the plants in the house have to be wiped clean so they shine. I'd say I have three hours of work for each of you this afternoon; then tomorrow morning you'll need to start cleaning the house itself."

Afraid the others might object, Becky quickly said, "We'll have to call home so our mothers know where we are."

"Why, of course!" Mrs. Llewellyn exclaimed. "But do it

quickly, dears. I was on the verge of calling a cleaning service, but the phone's been ringing so madly, I haven't had a chance. Are you sure you girls can wash windows and floors—and bathrooms?"

Jess wrinkled her nose. "*Bathrooms?* Uh . . . we only—"

"I need the whole house cleaned," Mrs. Llewellyn interrupted. "I also need people to serve at the party tomorrow night, and clean up afterward. I'm willing to pay you well, girls—a very high wage, actually." When she mentioned how much it would be per hour, Becky's eyes nearly popped out.

"Of course, for that kind of wage," she continued, "I expect good work. I'm sure you are good workers, or Mr. Bradshaw wouldn't have recommended you so highly."

"He recommended us highly?" Becky asked.

Mrs. Llewellyn smiled and chattered on.

It's a lot of money, Becky thought. "I'll clean the bathrooms tomorrow," she offered, so no one would back out. "And I'll wash the china and crystal today."

After a moment, Tricia said, "All right."

Cara and Jess were slower to agree, but Becky called her mother at the office and got permission right away.

"It's two o'clock now," Mrs. Llewellyn said, sounding as though time were being wasted. "The crystal and china are all in these cabinets. We've been away, so things could be quite dusty."

Becky nodded, already taking stacks of dishes to the sink while Tricia called home. Cara offered to damp-wipe the plants, and Jess said she'd polish the silver.

As soon as all four of them had made their calls, the phone rang again and Mrs. Llewellyn jumped and laughed. "I'll pick it up in another room so I can hear myself think." After a minute, the girls heard her muffled chatter.

"So *that's* what eccentric means," Tricia laughed.

"She's a character, but I think she's all right," Becky decided as she began to wash the dishes.

"Whatever you do, don't drop this china," Tricia said. "It looks expensive."

"What do you think I am, a klutz?" Becky asked.

Tricia laughed. "I'm just not going to get behind you in case you get nervous and back up into my legs!"

Becky had to stop washing while she laughed. "I can't believe we fell into a job like this right away. And at such good pay."

"And with a view of her swimming pool and the Pacific Ocean right out the kitchen window," Tricia remarked. "Do you think she'll really pay us as much as she said?"

Nearby at the cooking island, Jess polished the silver. "We'd better be sure to get paid for today before we leave."

Mrs. Llewellyn must have hung up the phone, because it rang again, and she cried out, "Oh, no!" cackling with laughter. Between calls, she bustled into the kitchen with more instructions. "Isn't this great fun, girls?" she asked, not waiting for an answer. "Isn't it fun to have a party? I feel as though I were born for it!"

"Becky had a birthday party yesterday," Cara said.

"You did?" Mrs. Llewellyn asked. "Happy birthday to you, Becky! I'll have to give you a present."

"Oh, no, Mrs. Llewellyn," Becky protested, "that won't be necessary."

"Maybe presents for all of you if you do good work," she said, scurrying out of the room.

An hour later the kitchen windows were steamed up, and

Becky's new T-shirt and shorts were drenched. Cara had finished damp-wiping plant leaves and had come to help dry the dishes. "How many dishes are there, anyhow?"

"One hundred of each. I counted them," Becky told her, her hands already shriveled like prunes from the hot soapy water. Cara was drying as fast as she could, and mountains of plates still surrounded them. "One hundred dinner plates, salad plates, dessert plates, cups, and saucers. There'll be nearly a hundred guests, so she wants every last thing in the cabinets washed."

"Everything?" Cara asked.

"Everything," Becky answered.

"Well, it's her money," Cara said, getting down creamers, sugar bowls, and serving plates.

After a while, Mrs. Llewellyn bustled in again. "I think we should wash all of the copper pots and pans hanging from the ceiling, too. It wouldn't do to have the catering service notice dust on my pots. Why, everyone would know—oh, my land, there's the doorbell!"

Jess brought a plastic pan full of polished silverware for them to wash. "This is just the beginning of the silver!"

Later, Mrs. Llewellyn was on the hallway phone. "Yes, it's a western barbecue, so dress accordingly. There'll be a small country band, and I have the most *darling* girls to serve and clean up. Just darling."

Becky and Jess rolled their eyes at each other while Cara carried another stack of dusty dishes to be washed.

Mrs. Llewellyn continued, "I do believe I'll have the girls dress western style, too—denim skirts, white shirts, bandannas, and cowgirl hats."

"We have to dress western, too?" Cara whipped around,

her feet slipping on the wet floor.

"Cara!" Jess yelled. "Don't drop—"

Becky grabbed her wildly with soapy arms.

"Ufff!" Cara cried. "Ohhh!" Finally she gained her balance without dropping a plate.

Becky let out a deep breath. "Whew! For a second, I thought we'd have to work here the rest of our lives to pay for broken dishes."

Cara set the plates on the stainless steel counter. "You and me both! I think my heart stopped."

When they'd recovered, Tricia said, "This job is like playing scullery maids in a school play. Now I know how to act if I ever get a scullery maid part."

"I feel like we're in one of Tricia's crazier skits. If we could see ourselves, we'd probably die laughing," Jess said. "But if we did, Mrs. L. would think we'd gone crazy and cackle with us."

At five o'clock the girls had finally finished, and Mrs. Llewellyn took the phone off the hook. "See you tomorrow morning, dears—eight o'clock sharp. You should be finished by three to go home to rest. You'll need to wear denim skirts and white shirts for the party. Oh, and bright bandannas, and cowgirl hats and boots too."

Becky panicked. "We don't have cowgirl boots."

Mrs. Llewellyn peered at their feet over the tops of her thick glasses. Becky was suddenly self-conscious of her holey tennies. "What sizes do you wear?"

"Six," Becky answered.

"Five," Tricia and Cara said together.

"I only wear a four," Jess added, "but I have sturdy feet.

By the way, we hoped you'd be able to pay us now for today's work."

"Of course!" Mrs. Llewellyn said, then emitted a loud cackle. "I'm getting so forgetful!" She bustled off, then returned with her purse and paid them just what she'd promised.

Becky's damp hair hung in her face in ringlets, and her legs and back ached, but it didn't matter as she looked at the bills in her dishpan hands. If they got more jobs like this, she and her mother and sister wouldn't have to leave California. She spoke quickly before anyone could change their mind about returning. "Thanks, Mrs. Llewellyn. We'll see you tomorrow morning at eight. And you can count on us for the party."

"I will," Mrs. Llewellyn said. Her huge eyes searched theirs. "I'm putting my trust in you. I know you won't let me down. Why, young girls like you are the hope of our nation!"

Outside at their bikes, Cara looked up at the huge house and suddenly laughed. "I don't see how we can ever get this place all cleaned in time. And we've never served a party before. It'll be like a Laurel and Hardy movie!"

Becky tried not to laugh, especially out here where Mrs. Llewellyn might hear them. "We'll figure out a way. We'll figure it all out somehow."

———————

It was almost six o'clock when Becky arrived home. A note lay on the kitchen counter.

Becky,
Mr. Morelli wants ten pizza invitations by tomorrow noon.
Amanda and I have run out to get more candles, pepperoni,

*envelopes, and yellow poster board. Be home soon. Casserole
already in the oven.*

*Love,
Mom*

Becky read the note again to be sure of the number. *Ten
pizza party invitations! Ten!* The way things were going, it
looked like now would be the only chance to wash her hair
before tomorrow night.

She'd just finished blow-drying it when her mother and
Amanda returned. Mom called out in an excited voice, "I
bought plenty of supplies, including poster board—precut."

"Thanks!" Becky said. "I'd better get to work now, because we start work again for Mrs. Llewellyn at eight o'clock
tomorrow morning. I'll have to deliver the invitations from
there."

"I didn't put it all together when you phoned me at work,"
Mom said. "You're working for Mrs. Exley Llewellyn—Paul
invited me to her western-style party tomorrow night."

"Oh, no, you're not going!"

"I did accept his invitation. Don't you want me to be
there?"

Becky looked forlornly at her mother. "I guess it doesn't
matter. It's just that she wants us to help serve at the party,
too. There'll be loads of people, and we don't have a clue what
we're supposed to do."

"I'm sure she'll tell you, Becky."

"I suppose. She's *very* good at instructions." Becky pulled
down the blue birthday streamers from the chandelier. "I'll
work here at the table so I can be with you two."

"Can I have the st'eamers for my room?" Amanda asked.

"Why not?" Becky said, tossing the streamers to her sister. She headed for her own room for art supplies. Ten pizza invitations seemed like a lot to finish tonight, but she was determined to make every last one of them.

Back at the table she laid out her pencils, watercolors, ruler, and colored marking pens. First, she scored the middle of the poster boards with a paring knife so they'd bend neatly. Next, she sat down and sketched a big pizza on the front of each card.

Mom stepped from the kitchen, wearing an old shirt and shorts. "I'd be glad to help."

"Maybe you could slice and microwave the pepperoni circles. They have to be very dry, or they grease everything."

"I'll do it now. How much are you charging for the cards?"

When Becky told her, her mother gasped. "Good grief, that's twenty-five dollars to start!"

Becky nodded. "This time I'm giving the profits to you, because I'll have plenty of money for shoes from the jobs at Mrs. L.'s."

"Oh, Becky, I can't take your money."

"You're not *taking* it, Mom. It's for *our* expenses." She'd almost added, *so we don't have to move*, but caught herself. "Besides, you're working as hard as you can, so why shouldn't I?"

Mom gave her daughter a peculiar look across the kitchen counter, then set to work slicing pepperoni.

It was already dark by the time Becky was finishing the cards. Her mother helped print

YOU'RE INVITED TO A PARTY

and inside:

PLACE:
DATE:
TIME:

Becky asked, "Do you like Paul Bradshaw?"

"He's a nice man, that's all. Why do you ask?"

Becky shrugged, awfully glad her mom wasn't in love. She glued on the last of the candles. Their family would manage alone—and stay in California—if she had to kill herself working.

———

The next morning, Mrs. Llewellyn rushed about more excited than ever. "I knew I could depend on you girls. I knew it! I've written out a list of all the jobs that need to be done, so you can start right away."

She explained what was on the list, and they all set to work. Jess washed the outside of the windows; Cara washed the inside. Tricia dusted and vacuumed, and Becky cleaned the bathrooms and the kitchen.

Outside, gardeners mowed the lawns, pruned bushes, and swept the patio. Before long, a truckload of men arrived to set up a huge canvas tent on the back lawn, then filled it with round white tables and matching chairs. A florist delivered a ton of flowers, and other delivery people arrived, one after the other. A woman Mrs. L. called a personal shopper brought white western outfits for the Llewellyns to wear for the party.

"Isn't this fun, girls?" Mrs. Llewellyn said as she rushed

from the doors to the phones. "Isn't this fun!"

A madhouse is more like it, Becky thought, polishing a bathtub on her hands and knees. She'd left the pizza invitations under her bike rack, waiting for just the right moment to get permission to leave and deliver them.

At eleven o'clock, Becky caught Mrs. Llewellyn between answering phones and doorbells. "I'm afraid I need to take off for a while to deliver some cards to Morelli's Pizza Parlor."

"Cards?" Mrs. Llewellyn asked. "Do you sell cards?"

"Actually, I do. I make them and sell them, but these are pizza party invitations—"

"Oh, pizza parties aren't for me, but I'd like to look at your other cards someday. You may go, but please hurry. There's still plenty of work to do."

Becky thanked her, wiped her hands, and headed for the back door. She'd left her bike in the shade, but the sun was shining on it now. Becky was appalled to find Lulu and two other dogs sniffing at the envelopes. "No!" she shouted. "Get away! Go home!"

They backed off a little, so she climbed on her bike and began to coast down the driveway, the distinct scent of pepperoni wafting in the breeze. The dogs were close behind, trotting hard after her and barking. "Stay!" Becky shouted over her shoulder. "Stay! Stay right here!"

The dogs paused for an instant, then bounded on behind her.

Becky turned onto Seaview Boulevard. "Home!" she shouted. "Home! Go home, dogs!"

Instead, the dogs barked louder, and two others joined in the chase.

Pedaling with all of her might out to Ocean Avenue, Becky

turned left, then sped downhill for Morelli's, the dogs barking and baying behind her like a pack of hunting dogs. Three or four more had joined in and were loping steadily alongside the crowded highway, ears back, tongues out.

Cars and trucks along the bike lane honked, and drivers gawked and yelled out. Suddenly, a van marked CHANNEL 10 TV swept into the lane beside Becky. She whirled to see a photographer filming her from the open sunroof.

At least nine dogs were in hot pursuit, like a chaotic circus parade, barking louder than ever. *"Go home!"* Becky shouted fiercely, pedaling faster and turning into the shopping strip's parking. *"Go home, you stupid dogs!"*

Someone stepped out of Flicks Video Store. "Look at that!" they shouted back inside, over the dogs' barking.

Cara's father peered out. "It's Becky Hamilton! Becky, what in the world are you doing?"

"Stop the dogs, please!" she cried, as a slobbery Saint Bernard snapped at the envelopes. She pedaled harder toward Morelli's bike rack, but she knew she didn't dare stop. "Get away! Get away!"

She circled the parking lot, the dogs still yapping at her heels. *Lord, help me!* she prayed. *Please help me!*

Suddenly a police car careened into the parking lot, its siren wailing above the uproar. Becky hoped he didn't mean for her to stop, because she couldn't. Siren still wailing, the officer tried to pull his car between her and the dogs, but the parking lot was jammed with cars, making it impossible. The police car was blocked, but not the dogs.

People came out of the stores to watch, and Mr. Morelli and his employees rushed out of their back door. "It's the pizza invitations!" he yelled. "Stop those dogs!"

The Channel 10 TV photographer jumped out of his van, filming with his video camera as he ran alongside Becky. People shouted from everywhere, and one man even flapped a blanket at the dogs like a bullfighter, but it didn't stop them.

Panting, Becky pedaled around Morelli's again.

Mr. Morelli waved wildly. "Ride into the back door! I'll hold it open just till you're inside!"

Becky pedaled with all of her might, aiming for Morelli's open back door. She ducked her head just as her bike bounced over the threshold and into the kitchen, slamming a table against the wall while two pizza chefs jumped for their lives.

Finally coming to a halt, Becky stood shaking astride her bike.

"You're safe!" Mr. Morelli said, the back door closed behind him. "It was a close call, but you're safe."

Becky's legs were quivering so hard she had to brace herself against the wall. "I'm sorry. I'm so sorry! Look what I've done to your kitchen!"

"Nothing that can't be easily fixed and cleaned up," Mr. Morelli assured her. "You all right?"

She drew a deep breath. "I think so." She glanced behind her. "Thank goodness, the pizza party invitations are okay, too."

Mr. Morelli took them carefully from under the bike rack. "What a sight that was!" His belly began to shake as he laughed out loud. "That was the greatest pizza race I've ever seen! Even better than those crazy pizza-tossing contests they have back in Italy. You belong in the Guinness Book of World Records, at least!"

Becky could only imagine how it must have looked with the dogs chasing behind her, snapping at the pepperoni cards, and her pedaling with all her might—not to mention the police car and the TV station cameraman. Despite her embarrassment, she almost laughed herself.

Out front, the high school clerk yelled, "There's a crowd coming in here, Mr. Morelli—a police officer, a TV photographer and reporter, and someone from the *Santa Rosita Times!*"

"Come on," Mr. Morelli said to Becky, leaning her bike against the kitchen wall. "This may be the publicity chance of a lifetime!"

A crowd gathered in front of the cash register, and Becky stayed close behind Mr. Morelli.

"What's this all about?" the police officer asked.

Mr. Morelli smiled. "This young lady was trying to deliver some pizza party invitations that we sell here. Like this sample on the counter," he said, pointing to it. "I'd guess those dogs smelled the real pepperoni and wanted to get their teeth into it in the worst way."

The TV reporter spoke to the photographer. "Take more footage of the girl. And get a shot of those invitations. It's a good human interest story. *Dogs Chase Pizza Invitations.*" She laughed. "What's your name?" she asked Becky. "And can you tell us exactly what happened?"

"I'm Becky Hamilton," she said nervously. Then she explained as best she could, telling about making the pizza invitations with real pepperoni for her own party, and then for Mr. Morelli to sell in his shop. She told about working for Mrs. Llewellyn, and about the dogs following her from there. She said that she prayed when the dogs chased her, for protection and a way to get the invitations delivered safely. She even explained about the Twelve Candles Club.

The *Santa Rosita Times* reporter told Mr. Morelli, "You must have mighty fine pizza here to get such a—" he chuckled, "—fine following."

"We do," Mr. Morelli said, trying not to laugh out loud on camera. "We have the best pizza in town."

"My family thinks so, too," Becky added.

It seemed forever before she'd answered all the reporters' questions, but at last they left, and Becky rushed back to Morelli's kitchen to get her bike. Fortunately, when she pushed it through the back door, Lulu Llewellyn and the other dogs were gone.

Mr. Morelli's check for $25 was in her pocket, but Becky feared she'd been gone so long that Mrs. Llewellyn would be furious. Hadn't she said over and over how much she was counting on all of them?

When Becky arrived, Mrs. Llewellyn shouted, "Becky! You're going to be on the noon news! They just said, 'Santa Rosita's own Becky Hamilton delivers pizza invitations that turn into a nine-dog circus. Stay tuned!' What on earth happened?"

Becky huffed and puffed, breathless from her hurried ride back. "I'll bet your Lulu's on the news, too."

"My Lulu?" Mrs. Llewellyn echoed. "On the news?"

Becky nodded, unsure what her employer might say.

"You'll both be celebrities!" Mrs. Llewellyn exclaimed. "Wait till I tell everyone! Oh, what a day to have a party!"

CHAPTER

5

Becky hurried along behind Mrs. Llewellyn to the den and found her friends gathered around the television set. "Becky!" Tricia yelled, "you're going to be on TV!"

"That's what I hear," Becky said uneasily.

"Lulu, too!" Mrs. Llewellyn settled Lulu on a cushion by the TV. "I'm going to videotape it for posterity."

Becky joined her friends on the floor, wondering how they would get all the cleaning done if they were watching TV.

Mrs. Llewellyn perched herself on the edge of the leather couch. "I'd just come in to catch the noon news when they mentioned your name, Becky. I do hope it tapes all right."

On the screen, a denture adhesive commercial promised to put excitement back into people's lives. Becky laughed. "If they want excitement, they ought to ride through town with pepperoni strapped to their bikes!"

The news anchorperson came on. "And now the local news.

We have an unusual story to tell you about a neighborhood chase. Becky Hamilton was delivering hand-made pizza invitations, and turned the event into a nine-dog circus! Here's Cindy with on-the-scene coverage."

To Becky's horror she saw herself riding across the TV screen on her bike, dogs of all sizes barking and yapping behind her. Then she heard the voice of the reporter who had inter-viewed her. "Twelve-year-old Becky Hamilton, of Santa Rosita Estates, rode her bike through town this morning to deliver pizza party invitations to Morelli's Pizza Parlor. Little did she dream that the smell of sun-warmed pepperoni on the invita-tions would lure the dogs of Seaview Boulevard to follow. . . ."

A close-up of the hungry pack of dogs, including Mrs. L.'s Lulu, flashed on the screen. Lulu rose from her cushion and barked at her image.

Mrs. Llewellyn gave a laugh. "Lulu Llewellyn, you might be famous for this, but you were a *very bad girl*."

Lulu lowered her head and wagged her stub of a tail.

Then Becky saw herself on the screen again, riding furi-ously through the shopping parking lot, police siren wailing while the officer tried to maneuver his car between her and the dogs.

The reporter continued, "Despite the efforts of our police department and bystanders . . ." They showed the man flap-ping a blanket like a bullfighter, and Mr. Hernandez and the others shouting and waving their fists at the dogs. ". . . noth-ing helped until Becky rode her bike around to the back door of Morelli's Pizza Parlor and straight into the kitchen."

Now Becky's face filled the screen. She was standing behind Morelli's counter by the cash register explaining about how she made the pizza party invitations. The camera zoomed in on the sample invitation on the counter.

"Were you scared when the dogs were chasing you?" the reporter asked.

"I sure was," Becky answered. "I prayed like everything!"

"Why were the dogs from Seaview Boulevard chasing you?" she asked. "You don't live there."

"I was there with my friends, the Twelve Candles Club, cleaning house for Mrs. Llewellyn."

"Mrs. *Exley* Llewellyn?"

Becky nodded. "Yes."

"Besides making pizza party invitations, you clean houses too?" the reporter asked.

Becky nodded. "The Twelve Candles Club helps at parties, does housecleaning, car washing, and we're starting Morning Fun for Kids next week. I make greeting cards too."

"You're a very busy young lady," the reporter said.

Becky nodded, looking bushed.

"What exactly is the Twelve Candles Club?"

"We're four girls, all twelve years old, and we want to work this summer to earn some extra money."

"How do you get these jobs?" she asked.

"Well, we put those free ads for summer jobs in the *Santa Rosita Times*, but they won't be out until Monday—"

The reporter from the newspaper interrupted. "Do you have a phone number where viewers can reach the Twelve Candles Club?"

Becky heard herself repeating Jess's number very slowly and clearly.

"Wow!" Jess said. "I'll bet my answering machine tape will be filled up!"

The interview ended with the newspaper reporter saying

to Mr. Morelli, "You must have mighty fine pizza here to get such a—" He laughed. "—fine following."

"We do," Mr. Morelli answered, smiling. "We think we have the best pizza in town."

"My family thinks so, too," Becky heard herself add.

The reporter's face filled the screen. "And there you have it. The story of a frightening chase and an exciting rescue— the story of a girl and her friends who are just out of school for summer vacation and already hard at work. We salute you, Becky Hamilton, and the Twelve Candles Club."

Mrs. Llewellyn beamed. "It'll be the talk of our party tonight, especially if they replay it on the evening newscasts. I do think I'll phone Mr. Morelli and order two pizzas right now for our lunch."

———

Despite the delay, by three o'clock the house gleamed, and the girls rode their bikes home to rest. Passing Morelli's, they noticed that the parking spaces around it were full to capacity.

When they arrived back at Santa Rosita Estates, Jess wanted to stop to see if there were any messages on her answering machine, but Becky was too tired. "We can worry about that later," she said. She could hardly wait to get home and lie down on her bed.

In her room, she'd no more than put her head on the pillow when she drifted off to sleep. Weird dreams filled her head: Dogs chased her downhill. She rode into Morelli's kitchen, which suddenly became an endless tunnel. The dogs chased her right inside. And the party at Mrs. Llewellyn's was a disaster. Becky dropped a tray of appetizers all over the guests.

Suddenly she felt a hand pat her shoulder. "It's five-thirty,

70

Becky," her mother said. "Time to get dressed for Mrs. Llewellyn's party."

Becky blinked groggily, incredulous that she'd slept for two hours. Her mother gazed at her wide-eyed. "Tricia told me you were on television. Something about you and a dog chase on the noon news!"

Becky nodded. "Right! I'll explain later. I've got to be at Mrs. Llewellyn's by six-thirty!"

"Let's turn on the TV," her mom said. "Maybe they'll show it again. I left Amanda at Gram's for the night. I told Tricia I'd drive you all home after the party, since I'll be there anyway."

The six o'clock news repeated the interview with Becky. When the dogs chased across the screen, the Hamiltons' dog, Lass, barked at the TV. For Becky, the strange thing about seeing the coverage again was that it looked plain wacko.

"I do believe Lass is sorry to have missed the chase," Mrs. Hamilton said. "I'm glad it turned out all right, Becky, but from now on, I trust you won't let your pizza party invitations sit out in the sun." She laughed and gave her daughter a hug.

"I won't, believe me! I never want to go through something like that again!"

After getting dressed, Becky phoned Jess. "Did you see it again?"

Jess laughed. "Yes! And our answering machine was *full*, and the phone's been ringing all afternoon. Are you ready to go?"

"I'm ready." Becky wore a white shirt, her new denim skirt, and her holey tennies. She didn't look like a cowgirl, but Mrs. Llewellyn said she would order cowboy hats and red bandannas for them. That would help a lot.

The moment Becky hung up the phone it rang again. Her mother got it. "Yes, I'm Becky's mother." Her blue-green eyes widened as she listened carefully. "Why, yes, it is. No, I don't." After a while, she added, "You have my approval, but let me ask Becky. Please don't give our address. Just one moment."

She held the receiver against her shoulder. "It's the *Santa Rosita Times*. They want to run an article about you in tomorrow's paper with the pictures they've already taken. Another reporter wants to talk to you for a Monday feature about their free ads for kids. They want to take pictures of all you girls working. What do you think?"

"I guess we ought to, especially since they're giving us free ads," Becky decided. "Maybe it would help us to get more jobs, too."

"Probably. What about the working pictures?"

Becky shrugged. "Tonight at Mrs. Llewellyn's?"

Mom spoke to the caller again. "They'll all be working at a party tonight at Mrs. Llewellyn's. You'll have to get permission from her as well as the other parents. Otherwise, it's okay with Becky and me."

After she hung up, Mom shook her head. "What a day! And it's only the second day of summer vacation!"

Mrs. McColl dropped the girls off at the Llewellyn home at exactly six-thirty. Even from the front yard they could smell the mouth-watering aroma of chicken and beef being barbecued out back.

The four hurried around the house. "How perfect everything looks!" Becky exclaimed. The huge white tent was filled with round tables covered with red-and-white-checked table-cloths and red geranium centerpieces. Caterers bustled about, busily setting food out in huge stainless steel warming pans. Every tree, shrub, and flowering bush in the yard was perfectly trimmed.

A short, gray-haired man in a crisp white western outfit hurried toward the girls. "You must be the famous Twelve Candles Club I've been hearing so much about. I'm Exley Llewellyn," he said, extending his hand and shaking theirs heartily.

"Mrs. Llewellyn is still getting ready," he told them. "Your bandannas and hats are in the laundry room downstairs," he said. "I think my wife has another surprise there for you, too. When you're all ready, the caterer, Mrs. Wurtzel, will tell you what to do."

The girls trooped to the laundry room to find four western hats and four red bandannas on the washer and dryer. Next to the machines stood four pairs of brand-new cowboy boots.

"Wow! Do you think these boots are for us?" Tricia asked.

"Sure," Jess said. "Remember, Mrs. L. asked for our shoe sizes. Look, they have high heels! What if we can't walk in them? How will we serve?"

"They're not too high," Tricia said. "If other people can work in heeled boots, so can we."

Laughing as they tied the bandannas around their necks and put on the big hats, the girls gingerly pulled on the boots and scrutinized one another. "We really look good!" Tricia said with a giggle. "All we need are ropes and horses, and we could ride off into the sunset!"

The five-man country band was just arriving with their instruments when the girls stepped into the backyard. Becky led the way to the long buffet table where the caterers were setting up the food. A dark-haired woman looked at them critically from across the table. "You girls must be the Twelve Candles Club. You'd better get over here right away for your instructions."

"Nice to meet you, Mrs. Wurtzel," Jess said, then muttered under her breath, "She sure looks like a grump."

"Hummmph," Mrs. Wurtzel said. She added, "Wurtzel Caterin' is known fer good food *and service*. Don't mess up. Usually we got trained women to serve our meals, but at the last minute Mrs. Llewellyn says we're usin' *twelve-year-old girls*. Don't mess up, you hear?"

Becky swallowed hard. *Maybe working at this party won't be as much fun as we thought.*

"We won't let you down," Jess promised. "Or the Llewellyns."

"Better not," the woman replied, glaring at them with steel-gray eyes. Then in rapid-fire fashion she began drilling them on serving and cleaning up. They were to offer appetizers as the guests milled around, keep ice water in all the glasses during dinner, make sure guests had all the food they wanted, while making certain everything on the tables and lawn was kept neat and clean and orderly. Afterward, while guests visited, they were to unobtrusively clean up the tables and yard, and wash all of the dishes by hand and put them away. The kitchen must be left spotless.

Just before seven o'clock, the band struck up a twangy western tune as Mrs. Llewellyn stepped out onto the veranda with the first guests. She wore a fringed white western-style dress, white western hat atop her frizzy red hair, and white high-heeled boots.

"Edith Llewellyn, you've outdone yourself again!" one of her guests enthused. "I half expect cowboys on horseback and a great herd of cattle to emerge from behind the tent. Actually, nothing would surprise me at one of your parties."

Mrs. Llewellyn cackled delightedly. "Well, it is different than last year's ancient Greek theme. No one seems to do western barbecues anymore, and I so enjoyed them back home in Texas when I was a girl."

Just then, Mrs. L. spotted the girls. "Oh, my dears, don't you look absolutely perfect!" She whirled to guests at the nearest table. "This is our own Becky Hamilton who was on the Channel 10 news today with my Lulu. I do hope all of you saw the coverage. It was so exciting! My poor darling Lulu is still exhausted from it all. She's resting in my bedroom this very minute."

Becky stifled a laugh and picked up a tray of shrimp appetizers. From the corner of her eye she could see the ever-present head-caterer staring at her. As politely as she could, she said, "May I offer you some shrimp, ma'am?"

"Why, yes, how sweet!" one of the guests gushed. She was a tall, scrawny-looking woman, dressed in a fringed, blue western dress. "Don't you look adorable! What a day you must have had with that television interview and all. Why, the last time I was on TV, I had to spend the day having my face and hair done. But of course," she said, suddenly embarrassed, "you wouldn't have time to prepare for a news story."

Becky managed to keep a neat smile on her face as she offered appetizers to everyone at the table. She noticed more and more guests arriving, but couldn't spot her mother and Paul Bradshaw in the crowd.

By seven-thirty the girls were going full tilt, serving appetizers, pouring water, and helping to serve from the buffet. The high-heeled boots, while fun to wear at first, were now beginning to take their toll in aching leg muscles and sore feet.

The country band kept the atmosphere light with such songs as "Okie From Muskogee." Becky didn't know much about country music, but she was beginning to like it. She moved as fast as she could, serving guacamole and tortilla chips, more shrimp and crab legs, while snatching up discarded napkins from the yard and tables, and clearing dirty china and crystal.

She'd completely forgotten about the phone call from the reporter at the *Santa Rosita Times*, until she heard Mrs. Llewellyn call out, "Girls, it's time for a picture of all of you with Mr. Llewellyn and me. Bring your serving trays with you. We want the readers to see what good workers you are."

Becky's face flushed as she straightened her bandanna and hurried over to join the others. She could tell by the look on Mrs. Wurtzel's face that she did not approve of pictures being taken in the middle of the party.

The newspaper reporter asked the usual umpteen questions while the photographer snapped pictures. Then the reporter asked in a serious tone, "Do you girls charge to work at benefits?"

Becky glanced at Tricia, then at Cara and Jess. They were no help, so she answered nervously, "Uh—this is the first party we've worked at, except for at home, of course."

Grinning, the reporter made a note of it and said no more.

The photographer turned to snap candid pictures of guests while Becky whispered to Mrs. Llewellyn, "What's a benefit?"

Thankfully, Mrs. Llewellyn spoke in a low voice. "The guests tonight have all given checks to Casa de Amparo. This party is a benefit to raise money for the battered children's home."

Becky's eyes widened in understanding as she looked at her friends. She was the leader of the Twelve Candles Club. They probably counted on her to make a decision here. For an instant she remembered how badly she and her mother needed the money if they were going to be able to stay in California. But then she thought about the battered kids. They didn't even have a happy home. She and her mom and sister might not have much money, but they had one another, and they had love in their home.

"Maybe we shouldn't charge for tonight," Becky blurted.

"It's fine with me," Tricia said without hesitation. "I'd be glad to help those kids."

Becky was impressed with her best friend's decision. She knew that she had family troubles herself—big ones.

"I'd like to give my earnings, too," Cara said matter-of-factly.

"Count me in," Jess added.

Mrs. Llewellyn held up a hand. "You girls are certainly big-hearted, but you have already worked very hard here to-night. If you donate half your earnings, you would be more than generous."

They looked at one another, surprised and elated at the same time. They nodded their agreement.

Becky turned to the reporter, who she was sure had not heard their conversation. "Our club is giving half our earnings tonight for the battered children."

The reporter dutifully made note of Becky's statement.

As Becky turned to resume serving the guests, she bumped into her mother and Paul Bradshaw. She wondered for a second if her mother would think she was crazy to have offered half her earnings. But when she quickly told her of their decision, her mother beamed with pride and hugged her, making Becky feel both embarrassed and good.

Mrs. Llewellyn tapped Becky on the shoulder and whispered, "I'm proud of all you girls. And I know you can keep a secret. You see, the reason I'm giving this party is that I was a battered child myself."

Becky gulped and looked at Mrs. L. hard. All the time she'd thought Mrs. Llewellyn was just a rich person who liked to throw parties to impress her friends. So much for judging.

She remembered Reverend Iddings, whom they called Bear, had once spoken of people having deeply hidden hurts. He'd told them to let their lights shine, to reflect God's love to others so others would find joy and hope. That's just what she'd do the rest of this evening, Becky decided. She'd trust in the Lord and work as hard as she could for the battered kids as well as for Mrs. Llewellyn's guests.

She even managed to smile sincerely at Mrs. Wurtzel while she waited on tables. Anyone who looked as grouchy as she did was sure to have some serious problems. Maybe God could even use Becky Hamilton to help an old grump.

CHAPTER

6

At breakfast the next morning, Mom handed a section of the *Santa Rosita Times* to Becky. "Read all about Becky Hamilton's wild escape from pepperoni-crazed dogs!" she announced in her best broadcaster's voice.

Becky looked uneasily at the newspaper over the box of cereal. At least she was pictured standing behind Mr. Morelli's counter, instead of wildly pedaling her bike in front of a pack of dogs. Apart from the fact that her hair needed brushing, it wasn't a bad picture.

"Can you make five pizza party invitations this morning?" her mother asked. "Mr. Morelli called after you left last night. He needs them by one o'clock, and I told him I thought you could manage it. There are enough supplies, but at the rate things are going, we'd better buy more."

Becky gulped down her orange juice. "I'll start right away. I'm going to make Mr. Morelli a pizza birthday card as a present, too."

"How nice, Beck. How about if this time, *I* drop them off at Morelli's while I'm out doing errands?"

"Great idea," Becky answered, smiling at her mother.

After breakfast, Becky gathered supplies from her room and brought them back to the dining room table to begin. As she worked, she could hear the familiar hum of the washing machine and dryer. Somehow, it was the comforting sound of a typical Saturday morning at home.

An hour later, Becky had almost completed the invitations. "Either they're getting easier to make, or I'm getting faster," she told her mother.

"That's good news," Mom remarked.

Just as Becky was thinking that she'd soon be $12.50 richer, her mother asked, "What's that burning smell?" Running into the laundry room, she called out, "It's the washing machine! The motor's going and the wash water is overflowing! Grab some rags, Becky. Hurry!"

Bringing the rags from under the kitchen sink, Becky raced to the laundry room. "What a mess!" The machine had stopped, but water covered the floor and was running out the back door.

"I knew this old thing was giving out," Mom moaned, sweeping the water out with a broom, "but I'd hoped it would hold on until we'd decided about moving."

Becky cringed at the mere thought of moving, and quickly asked, "How much for a new washing machine?"

Her mother drew a deep breath. "Between three hundred and eight hundred dollars. And the dryer has a strange roar to it, too."

As Becky mopped around the machine with an old towel, she offered, "Well, you already have a hundred dollars toward it, Mom. You can have my birthday check for twenty-five dollars and the seventy-five dollars I've already earned from working. I'll be making plenty more, and I really want to help."

"That's very generous of you, Beck, but let's save your money for shoes and clothes. We don't know if you'll continue to make that much money all summer. We can manage without a washing machine for now."

"Can't you charge a new one?"

Still sweeping out the water, Mom brushed her hair back with her arm. "We can't afford to charge anything. Unless you pay the amount in full when it comes due, you pay a big monthly interest charge. And if we move, I don't want to add a new machine to the cost of moving."

"But, Mom, I don't *want* to move!"

"I don't want to, either, Becky," she said, holding her daughter close, "but sometimes it's necessary to do things we don't particularly want to do."

If only Dad were still alive, Becky thought. They'd never been rich, but they hadn't had money problems, either. *If only—no!* she told herself. If only's got her nowhere. She'd done enough of that kind of thinking for two years.

Finally they finished mopping up, and Mom dumped the wet clothes into plastic buckets. "I'll take them to Gram's to finish up, and after today we'll use a laundromat."

We just can't move away! Becky thought, as she finished up the pizza party invitations. *Lord, help me to know what to do*, she prayed.

She half-hoped God would boom out an answer, but there was only silence and the feeling that she should continue to work hard.

———

By eleven o'clock, Mom had returned from Gram's and talked Becky into riding along with her to Morelli's, then stopping at the Shoe Stall and Santa Rosita Stationers. At twelve-thirty, she dropped Becky off at home with more pizza card supplies and two new pairs of shoes: white sandals and white canvas tennies. Becky felt good about the fact that she had paid for everything with her own money.

"See you at dinner," Mom called as she backed her old yellow Dodge out the driveway.

The phone was ringing as Becky stepped into the house. She dropped her packages and picked it up. "Hello?"

It was Jess, and she rattled on faster than usual. "I'm leaving in a minute for the gymnastics meet, but I've answered some of our phone messages. Can you help Tricia clean at the Terhune's down the street? Cara's working at the video store."

"Sure," Becky said. "Right away?"

"One o'clock. Mrs. Terhune is coming home from the hospital with their new baby tomorrow, and Mr. T. wants the house clean. The pay's only half what Mrs. Llewellyn gave us."

"Guess we won't get paid that much in our neighborhood."

"Probably not," Jess agreed. "I gave Tricia a pile of fliers to stuff into mailboxes. Only for neighbors we know, of course. And we need to have a special meeting tonight to discuss all the phone calls. How about my house at six o'clock?"

"Sounds great. Have a good meet!"

Becky stashed her art supplies and new shoes in her room, then went to the kitchen to make a sandwich for lunch. Mom hadn't gotten groceries yet, and they were down to peanut butter and grape jelly. She slathered both on the bread, grabbed the house key, and was out the door.

"Tricia," she called at the stucco house next door, "let's go!" She watched the second-floor window, but there was no sign of her friend.

Then she came running out the garage door. "Coming!" She smiled, fliers in hand. "I tried to call you. Where've you been?"

"Shopping, and to Morelli's to deliver more invitations."

"What'd he say about yesterday's wacko delivery?"

Becky laughed. "He thought it was great. He's never had so much business."

"After what you went through, he ought to pay you for publicity," Tricia said.

"I'm just glad to be selling the cards. Besides, he told Mom to stop in for a free pizza tonight."

"Wow, that's something!" Tricia said.

"I made a pizza birthday card for him as a gift, and he liked it. It's his brother's birthday next week, so he put the card in the freezer!"

Tricia laughed. "It's no crazier than having pepperoni on a birthday card. He's all right."

Becky took a bite of her sandwich. "Hey, you're wearing your boots from Mrs. Llewellyn. How come?"

Tricia giggled. "I thought if I wore them, I'd feel like a cowgirl, and the cleaning wouldn't be so boring. Besides, it's good practice for wearing high-heeled shoes someday."

Becky poked her arm. "*You* are wacko!"

Tricia grinned, her chin in the air and her reddish-blond hair flying in the breeze.

"Are we going to have to baby-sit little Tina Terhune while we work? I forgot to ask Jess."

"No, Tina's staying with her aunt while her mom's in the

hospital," Tricia said. "Only cleaning drudgery today."

Becky smiled at her friend. "Yeah, but after working for Mrs. Llewellyn, this job will seem dull."

"After working for her, *anything* would be dull!"

They took turns stuffing fliers in the neighbors' mailboxes, getting rid of seven by the time they arrived at the Terhunes' Spanish-style, white house.

Mr. Terhune opened the front door as soon as they reached it. "Am I glad to see you girls!" he said. "I'm sorry, but the house is a mess. My wife hasn't felt up to doing much cleaning in the last month or so."

Mr. Terhune was a tall, thin man; even his face looked bony, but he had a nice smile. "I'll be running errands," he told them, "then stop to visit Mrs. T. and the baby at the hospital." He looked sheepish when he asked, "Can I talk you into cleaning the kitchen, too? I haven't had much time. After work every day I run to the hospital, and then visit Tina at her aunt's."

Becky looked at Tricia, who gave a small nod.

"Sure," Becky said. "The fliers say dusting, vacuuming, and window washing, but we're flexible." It was the same thing at Mrs. Llewellyn's. How could they turn down honest work? Without thinking, she asked, "Shall we do the bathrooms too? Not that I *like* to do them, but with the new baby and all—"

"I sure would appreciate it," Mr. Terhune said, looking truly grateful.

He showed the girls where to find the vacuum cleaner, dust cloths, and other cleaning supplies. The house was so much like Becky's, she felt she could have found the things without being told where they were.

After he left, Tricia said to Becky, "Let's really make this house shine. I've been thinking about what Gramp says about doing unto others as you'd have them do unto you. If I'd just had a baby, I guess I'd like to come home to a sparkling-clean house."

"Me too," Becky agreed. "That'll be our goal. Hey, let's turn on that country music station. We can pretend we're at Mrs. Llewellyn's."

Tricia laughed, and tuned in to the sound of "Neon Rainbow."

While Becky scrubbed the kitchen to the beat of the music, a brainstorm hit. *If Mom won't take any household money from me, I'll just add today's pay to the places where she hides "secret money." Mom's so busy, she'll never even notice.*

———————

"This meeting will now come to order," Jess said, sitting on the edge of her trampoline. As usual after a gymnastic meet, she looked a little beat.

"How did you do?" Becky asked, even though she didn't understand a lot about gymnastics.

Jess looked dejected and drew a deep breath. "I lost my concentration and goofed up on the beam. I don't even want to think about it. Let's start on business."

Jess's bedroom resembled a gym. It had been a three-car garage, remodeled into a huge room with a high-beamed ceiling and painted white. Besides twin beds, there was a chest of drawers and matching desk, floor mats, parallel bars, a small trampoline, a gymnast's beam, a ballet *barre* in front of a huge mirror, and enormous posters on the walls of Olympic gymnasts like Mary Lou Retton, Nadia Comaneci, and Julianne McNamara.

"Let's elect a president," Jess began. "And I'll say right off, that if we're going to use my phone, that's enough for me, especially if it's going to be like it has been the last few days. I don't want to be president."

"Then I nominate Becky," Cara said. "She's the one who had the idea in the first place for the Twelve Candles Club."

"Me?" Becky looked aghast. "I've never been a president of anything."

"Neither have we," Cara reminded her.

Becky swallowed. "I wouldn't know how to go about it."

"Don't you remember from Girl Scouts?" Jess asked.

Becky shook her head. "Not much."

"How to go about it isn't all that important," Tricia stated firmly. "But if you think it is, you could go to the library and get a book on conducting meetings. I second Cara's nomination. You'd be great Becky. You're not too bossy."

How could I be in charge without being bossy? Becky wondered. "I don't know . . . I'm not really a leader—"

"It's been moved and seconded that Becky be president of the Twelve Candles Club," Jess interrupted. "Any discussion?"

Cara and Tricia shook their heads.

"Since there's no discussion," Jess continued, "all for Becky Hamilton for president, say *aye*."

"*Aye*," the three chorused before Becky could refuse.

"Becky Hamilton is our president," Jess announced. "Okay, Beck, take over."

Becky rolled her eyes. "Thanks—I guess. What do I do next?"

"Open the floor for nominations for vice-president, secretary, and treasurer," Tricia said matter-of-factly. "Don't you remember *anything* from Girl Scouts?"

"What do we need a treasurer for?" Cara asked.

Becky shrugged. "To buy snacks for Morning Fun for Kids, and anything else we need to stay in business, plus split up the money we earn from joint efforts."

"I offer to be vice-president," Jess said, "in charge of phone calls and photocopying, but nothing else."

"I so move," Cara said.

That was easy. The others agreed, and before long they'd elected Cara as secretary, because she was their best writer, and Tricia as treasurer, because she was the only one left.

"I suppose we ought to make the name of the club official," Becky said. "Does anyone have any other suggestions?"

Jess laughed. "After what happened at Mrs. Llewellyn's, and your famed TV dog chase, maybe we ought to call it Club El Wacko."

Everyone laughed out loud, and Tricia slapped her knees. "I love it!"

"It doesn't sound serious enough," Cara objected, then grinned. "But we could call it Club El Wacko just among ourselves."

Becky tried not to laugh, because it didn't seem very presidential. "Any other suggestions?"

"If we're going to be serious," Tricia said, "I like the idea of letting our lights shine—like candles."

Cara eyed her as if she didn't quite understand. Finally, she said, "If it's okay with Jess, it's okay with me."

Jess nodded. "I like the sound of it—the Twelve Candles Club. And the initials TCC sound great too. Someone who called asked if there were twelve of us, and I thought, not yet, but who knows? Anyhow, it leaves room for more members."

So it was official. They were the Twelve Candles Club.

Becky suddenly remembered her Girl Scout business meetings. "Any old business?"

"The messages on my answering machine," Jess said. "We've got to call everyone back. I called a few I knew, like the Terhunes. Here's a copy of the list for each of us."

Becky looked at hers. There were twenty-one names, phone numbers, and notes about what they wanted done. "Why don't Cara, Tricia, and I split these up?" she said. "We can check their references and find out when they want help. Jess has done lots of work already, and she'll be getting more phone calls. We'll have to divide things up so it's easiest for everyone, and we all get the jobs we like best."

"You're already sounding presidential," Tricia teased. "You're a natural, Beck. I knew it. Tall girls look the part anyway."

"Oh, come on, Trish," Becky said, suddenly embarrassed.

After they'd split up the names to call back, they decided to meet again on Monday at eight, one hour before Morning Fun for Kids was to start.

Walking home with Tricia, Becky thought again about moving. Normally, it was never far from her thoughts, probably because deep down inside she wanted to forget it. As they neared her house, Becky noticed that Paul Bradshaw's navy blue Cadillac was parked in the driveway.

"Hmmm!" Tricia rolled her eyes at Becky. "Isn't that Mr. Bradshaw's car?"

"Never mind," Becky fussed. "I've got enough to worry about without *him*! See you tomorrow morning."

"Bye," Tricia said, turning into her own driveway.

Becky tried to sneak quietly into the house, and was unnerved to see her mother sitting with Mr. Bradshaw on the couch. They were watching a video. *At least they aren't sitting very close together*, she thought. It felt strange to see Mr. Bradshaw in her house alone with her mother. Mom must have invited him.

"Oh, there you are, Beck!" Mom called from the living room.

"Yeh," Becky said, trying to sound unconcerned. "Hi, Mr. Bradshaw."

"Hello, Becky," he said cheerily. "You girls did a fine job at Mrs. Llewellyn's."

"Thanks. Thanks for getting us the job, too."

"How did your first meeting go?" her mother asked.

"Oh, fine," Becky answered. "Everything went fine."

No sense discussing her concern about being elected president—or about moving, at least not right now. " 'Night, Mom. 'Night, Mr. Bradshaw," she said, hurrying to her room.

Suddenly the thought struck: *If we move away, how can I be president of the Twelve Candles Club?*

CHAPTER

7

On Sunday morning, Becky's family piled into the Bennetts' maroon mini-van to go to church. Becky felt special in her blue birthday dress, white coral necklace, and new white sandals. She was determined to set all her worries aside. After all, just a while ago, she'd managed to slip her extra change into Mom's change box and a twenty-dollar bill into the ice bucket, where Mom hid money she didn't want to carry in her billfold. That would help with expenses.

Becky's mother sat in the front seat of the mini-van with Tricia's mom, who was her good friend. Becky sat in the middle seat with her little sister, who was wearing the new yellow dress Gram had made. Though the style and color were different from Becky's, it was made of the same tiny-white-butterfly-print fabric. Tricia sat in the backseat between her five-year-old brother, Bryan, and seven-year-old sister, Suzanne, to keep them quiet.

As they drove off, Amanda stuck out her legs to show her

new white sandals. "Just like yours, Becky."

"No, they aren't! Mine aren't open-toed," Becky pointed out. Realizing she sounded indignant, she softened her tone. "They're both white, though."

Amanda nodded, satisfied. She was clutching a new brown stuffed rabbit named Buster Bunny. "Wasn't Mr. Bradshaw nice to give me Buster Bunny last night?"

"I guess so," Becky said, glancing out the window.

It was a beautiful sunny morning, and the palm trees swayed in the breeze. While Tricia tried to stop an argument between Bryan and Suzanne, her mother discussed her troubles with Mrs. Hamilton. She and her husband were separated, and Mr. Bennett lived in Los Angeles.

Then Mrs. Bennett changed the subject, and asked Becky's mom, "Have you decided yet about moving?"

Becky's brain went on full alert.

Mrs. Hamilton put her finger to her lips, and Mrs. Bennett said, "Sorry, Libby. I forgot."

Please, Lord, Becky prayed fervently, *please don't let us move!* When she opened her eyes she saw the palm trees again, and thought about the fact that if they moved to another state, she'd probably never even see palm trees again.

At Santa Rosita Community Church, Becky and Tricia headed for their Sunday school class. "You're so quiet, Beck. What's going on?"

"I shouldn't be president," Becky blurted. "It's not right, with us maybe moving away."

"It's fine," Tricia countered, "because we're going to make so much money that you won't have to move!"

"I don't know. . . ."

Tricia stuck her chin up. "Well, I do. You're not resigning and that's final!"

No sense discussing it when Tricia was being so *final*, Becky decided. Maybe it wouldn't hurt to stay president for now.

Just then, Bear, the youth pastor, passed the girls in the hall. "Good morning, ladies," he said with a broad smile that made his blue eyes twinkle. Bear's nickname came from the fact that he was short and stocky with broad shoulders, and looked like a teddy bear. His face glowed with the love of God. "Say, Becky, I saw you in the great chase on the TV news. I rooted for you all the way. And . . . I was happy to hear you say right on TV that you prayed when the dogs were chasing you."

Becky smiled, feeling a little embarrassed at the attention.

"Are you okay otherwise?" he asked.

Becky shrugged. Nothing that might be bothering her could be shared now, not with the crowd of people hurrying around them to classes and services.

"Hmmm," Bear said, a knowing look in his eyes. "Have you prayed about whatever's bothering you?"

Becky swallowed hard. "Ummm . . . yes."

He smiled. "Do you know the four ways that God answers prayer?"

"I guess I don't."

"Well, He says yes, no, later, or thought-you'd-never-ask."

Becky smiled at the last one. "I sure have been asking!"

"And what is God saying to you?"

"I think He might be saying *later*." She remembered the washing machine breaking down, and the dryer on its way out. "Things . . . are getting worse."

"I'll put you on my prayer list, Becky, and I'll send you a

little guide to prayer." Before he left them, Bear patted Becky on the head, something she normally detested, but somehow coming from Bear it was okay.

Tricia said, "Come on, we'll be late, and today I have to be in the church skit."

"Oh, doing what part?"

Tricia grinned. "Acting like a brat in a family drama."

"Shouldn't be too hard for you," Becky teased, making both of them laugh. "Or should I say, it'll be the world's greatest acting job?"

"Yeah," Tricia said, "that sounds better."

———

After church, Becky met her grandmother out front.

"Happy birthday, Becky Anne Hamilton!" Gram said, giving her granddaughter a big hug. "I'm so glad you're letting me take you out for a birthday brunch."

Becky squeezed her grandmother back, ignoring the smiles of the people around them. She felt safe in Gram's arms. "I love this new dress you made me, and the cute doll for my bed. You're the best grandmother in the whole world."

"In the whole world?" Gram echoed. "I'm glad to hear you think so." She looked extra pretty when she smiled. Her short brown hair was neatly curled and perfectly in place. She wore a soft blue-green dress, the same color as her eyes.

"Hey," Becky noticed suddenly, "your belt is made of the same butterfly print as my dress."

Her grandmother laughed lightly. "Yes, I love butterflies. They remind me of being born again."

"Oh, neat. I hadn't thought of that."

"It's the most important thing to know and be certain of."

"I know, Gram. You're right about that," Becky acknowledged. It was the one thing she knew for sure. She'd accepted Jesus Christ as her Savior and Lord two years ago. Even in the midst of all their troubles, she had joy because of Christ in her heart.

Gram stood back to get a better look at Becky's dress. "It looks even better on you than I'd hoped."

Becky gave a little whirl, making the skirt flare out, then looked around, hoping no one had noticed.

Her grandmother adjusted the stole on Becky's shoulders, then said, "I hear you're quite busy with your new club."

"Right! You should see all the jobs we're getting since I appeared on TV. It's amazing."

Gram shook her head and smiled. "I believe it. I almost fainted dead away when I saw you on the six o'clock news. I hope you never give me a shock like that again."

"Believe me, Gram, I didn't do it on purpose!"

"Oh, I know that," her grandmother laughed, hugging her again. "But isn't it a fine example of how God uses all things for the good of those who love Him and are called to His purpose?"

"I hadn't thought about it in quite that way," Becky admitted. "But it's exactly what we studied this morning in our Sunday school class."

"That's an interesting coincidence. Seeing life through God's eyes is the best way." She glanced toward the Spanish-style church building. "Here come your mother and Amanda. Now, where did I park my car?"

After a little searching she spotted her green Oldsmobile. Though not new, Becky thought it was a nice car. Her grandfather had left Gram "comfortable," as she called it, when he died ten years ago. And whenever she felt up to it, Gram took interior decorating jobs.

When Becky's mom and sister caught up to them, Gram gave Amanda a big hug. "Where did you get that handsome rabbit?"

"Mr. Bradshaw gave him to me last night," Amanda answered. "His name is Buster Bunny."

"Oh, really?" Gram remarked. "How nice of Mr. Bradshaw." She darted a questioning look at her daughter.

Mom avoided Gram's eyes and quickly changed the subject. "Let's go, I'm starved!"

Mom sat in the front seat with Gram, and Amanda and Becky climbed in the back. As they drove out of the church parking lot, Becky thought about the fact that her grandmother never said or asked much about Paul Bradshaw, however curious she might be.

When they arrived at the Beachcomber Restaurant, they found Gram had reserved a booth overlooking the ocean. It was a beautiful view, and Becky wished she'd brought her sketch pad along. The surface of the water sparkled in the bright sunlight, and white-fringed waves washed up tangles of seaweed onto the sandy shore. Sailboats in the far distance seemed to sail along the edge of the earth.

Becky thought that if she were to sketch the scene, she'd show it through the restaurant window, with plants hanging in the foreground. That way it wouldn't be just another ocean picture.

After they'd placed their orders, Gram said, "Tell me more about the Twelve Candles Club, Becky. I just know what I heard on TV."

Becky smiled, and pulled three folded fliers out of her white shoulder bag. "I knew you'd ask, so I brought these for you to give out to friends." She turned to her mother. "I forgot to tell you this morning that they elected me president of the club."

"President?" Her mother looked impressed. "How nice."

Becky nodded, feeling uncertain again about the job.

"You'll make a fine president, Becky," her grandmother said. "You're a go-getter, just like your mother."

Mom closed her eyes for an instant, as if she were embarrassed by Gram's comment. "I don't know about that. My ex-boss's job has been open for two months, but I don't seem to have the courage to apply for it."

"Why on earth not?" Gram asked.

"Partly because I've never been an account executive. I don't have any experience." Mom looked out at the ocean. "Besides, I'd have to travel a few days out of every month."

"You'd be good at that, Libby," Gram said. "And I'd be glad to stay at the house with the girls. You know I like to help."

"You already help us so much," Mom said. "I don't want to impose on you. I really shouldn't have mentioned it. The whole idea makes me nervous. With house payments and new taxes, the only sensible thing to do is to—" She broke off her sentence and looked out at the ocean again.

Becky knew what her mother had almost said. *The only sensible thing to do is to move somewhere less expensive.*

Just then, the waitress brought omelettes for Gram and Mom, and waffles and sausage for Becky and Amanda. Gram bowed her head and gave thanks for the food, adding a request for wisdom and guidance for her daughter.

While they ate, Gram said, "Before I forget, Becky, I've

got an order for ten of your sparkly shell-stamped cards. A friend of mine is having a beach party. She wants 'It's a beach party!' on the front and 'Place, Date, and Time' inside."

Becky's spirits soared. "Those are my favorites to make. I'll work on them tomorrow afternoon." The new order seemed to Becky like another proof that she'd be able to earn enough money so they wouldn't have to move away.

She was just thinking about what a wonderful birthday brunch it had been with her family when waiters and waitresses arrived with a small chocolate cake lit with twelve candles. They sang a rousing version of "Happy Birthday," and everyone in the restaurant seemed to turn and look their way. She hoped they wouldn't recognize her from the dog chase on TV.

As soon as they arrived home, Becky phoned the seven people on her list from Jess's answering machine. Everyone was happy to provide references. One of them was her former second-grade teacher, Mrs. Davis. Nearly everyone had called about the Morning Fun for Kids.

"We start tomorrow," Becky told them, giving the details. "We're going to make it lots of fun for little kids."

At least that is what she and the rest of her friends hoped.

————

Early Monday morning, Becky hurried over to Tricia's with Amanda in tow. As president, Becky felt it was best to be early, even though she and Tricia had phoned each other umpteen times the night before. They had decided to each donate three dollars to the treasury, so Tricia could buy balloons and mid-morning snacks for the week. Tricia in turn would pay Becky for any craft supplies she had to purchase. For today, they'd make duck puppets out of construction paper and popsicle sticks.

"Please be good," Becky cautioned Amanda. "Cara and Jess don't have little sisters or brothers, and they don't know what a pain—I mean, how *active* little kids can be. They might want to quit Morning Fun for Kids after our very first morning."

Amanda pursed her lips in a pout.

Becky had lettered a yellow poster with the words

MORNING FUN FOR KIDS PLEASE KNOCK ON GATE

She taped it to the Bennetts' side gate, then reached over to undo the latch. She was glad she could barely reach it, because she knew it would be safe for the little kids.

"Amanda and I are here!" she called out to Tricia from the breezeway. She'd been at the Bennetts' thousands of times, but this morning she looked at the backyard with Morning Fun for Kids in mind.

There was a colorful gym set and sandbox, a tree house in the California pepper tree, and a solid wooden fence around the yard. They could do their crafts on the redwood picnic table, and the clay tile water fountain in the breezeway would be great for thirsty kids. There was even a passthrough shelf from the kitchen window, which would help for serving snacks, and where Butterscotch, the Bennetts' old cat, sat like a princess surveying the busyness around her. Even the fresh peach color of the two-story house made the setting look cheerful and welcoming.

Tricia came out the back door just as Mrs. Bennett opened the kitchen window. "I picked up some big cardboard boxes at the supermarket," she said. "Kids love to play in them."

"We don't even know how many kids will come," Tricia said, "besides Amanda and Bryan and Suzanne."

"Well, Mrs. Davis is bringing her four-year-old twin boys," Becky told them. "And a lot of other mothers were interested."

Tricia crossed her eyes. "I've heard those Davis twins are real terrors. We'd better get the morning's activities planned. I borrowed a book from the library that's full of ideas."

Amanda wore a green-and-white play dress with tiny red strawberry appliques. She looked adorable, except for the frown on her face when she asked, "What'll *I* do?"

"Why don't you go inside and play with Bryan for now," Tricia suggested.

Amanda looked disappointed. "I thought this was gonna be fun!"

"It will be," Becky promised. "Morning Fun for Kids will be more fun than anyone has ever dreamed. But you're the first one to arrive besides Bryan and Suzanne. It doesn't start till nine o'clock. And because none of you three are paying to come, you may all have to help us."

Amanda trudged into the Bennett house, turning back to glare at her sister, "Tell us when it's nine o'clock!"

"We will," Becky assured her.

"Don't let Chessie out of the house!" Tricia called out after her about their golden retriever.

Minutes later, when Jess and Cara arrived, the girls made their final decisions as to what everyone would do on this first morning. Cara, as secretary, wrote:

AFTER PARENTS SIGN THE KIDS IN:
1. *Magic carpet (Tricia. Rest of us blow up balloons and make foil balls)*
2. *Foil ball game (Becky)*
3. *Balloon fun (Jess)*
4. *Mid-morning snacks (Cara)*
5. *Gymnastics (Jess)*
6. *Free time for swings, etc. (all in charge)*
7. *Crafts (Becky)*
8. *Sand castle contest (all in charge)*

It sounded like plenty to do for three hours. They decided to call the kids "funners," because most kids didn't like being called kids or children. They would make the morning so much fun that the funners would beg to come back again.

Just before nine o'clock, a car pulled up in front of the house.

"Our first paying funners!" Becky cheered. "Where's that sign-in clipboard?" She found it on the picnic table, and hurried to the breezeway gate. It had been decided that as president, it was Becky's job to greet the first arrivals. Jess would greet the next, then Tricia, then Cara. That way, everyone would be welcomed by one of the "fun-makers."

There was a knock on the gate, and Becky quickly unlatched it. Mrs. Davis stood smiling with her four-year-old twins.

Becky swallowed. "Good morning. Welcome to Morning Fun for Kids! We'd like parents to sign in their children—we're going to call them funners—on the clipboard each morning, and sign them out at noon."

"Good idea," Mrs. Davis said. "These are my boys, Joe and Jim. We call them Jojo and Jimjim."

Becky wanted to giggle, but said in her best grown-up voice, "Hello, Jojo and Jimjim." The boys looked exactly alike dressed in their bright green playsuits. They were cute kids, with green eyes, dark curly hair, and freckled noses. Becky noticed an excited glint in their eyes when they spotted the swings and slide.

"Swings!" one shouted, and the two bolted for the backyard.

Mrs. Davis laughed. "I do believe they'll enjoy it here. They're alone together so much that it will be good for them to play with other children. Like most identical twins, they sometimes use a secret language, but you'll get used to it." She took the clipboard and pencil, and began to fill in the form Mrs. Bennett had helped the girls work out: FUNNER'S NAME, AGE, TIME IN, TIME OUT, PARENTS' PHONE, DOCTOR'S NAME/PHONE NUMBER. Then Becky handed Mrs. Davis two name tags for each of the boys, to be worn on the front of their shirt and on the back.

Becky heard two more cars pull up and voices coming from the sidewalk. While Mrs. Davis filled out the form, she motioned for Jess to tend the gate.

Mrs. Davis asked to look around the backyard and to talk to Mrs. Bennett, taking extra time no one had counted on. Becky passed the clipboard to Jess, and took Mrs. Davis to the back while more cars pulled up in front.

"Go! Go!" Jojo and Jimjim yelled as Cara pushed them as fast as she could on the swings. Between the "go-go's" they shrieked something like, "Umpty-dumpty-um-dum-a-lum."

Mrs. Davis knew Mrs. Bennett from second-grade parent-teachers meetings, but Becky guessed she wanted to be sure there'd be a parent around.

It was Cara's turn to greet newcomers at the gate, and Becky ran to the twins, certain they must be terrified of swinging so high. "You want me to stop the swings?"

"Umpty-dumpty-um-dum-dum!" they shrieked happily.

Becky guessed it must be their secret language.

Amanda came out into the yard with Bryan and Suzanne. "You said you'd tell us when the fun started," Suzanne complained.

"Everyone's not here *yet*," Becky told them, "but you can come out anyhow."

"Becky, you're next to greet parents!" Cara called out, panicking.

The yard was filling up fast with mothers, one father, and lots of excited kids. Jess, Tricia, and Cara were each busy either signing someone in or showing parents and kids around.

Becky greeted a mother at the gate, and her boy demanded, "I want to see the girl who walks on her hands!"

"That's Jess," Becky said, smiling. "She'll show you how it's done later."

"We saw you at Seaview Park," the mother said, "and Craig hasn't stopped talking since about the girl who walked upside-down."

"We're glad you came," Becky said. Out front she could hear more car doors slam, and in back the Davis twins continued to shriek, "Umpty-dumpty-um-dum-a-lum! Umpty-dumpty-um-dum-dum!"

Becky had a feeling this morning was going to be just plain wacko. *Umpty-dumpty-um-dum-a-lum!* she thought to herself.

CHAPTER

8

By nine-fifteen, twelve little kids filled the yard, including Amanda, and Bryan and Suzanne Bennett. Becky whispered to Tricia, "Looks like plenty for the first morning. Let's hope no more come."

"You know it," Tricia said. As they rolled out a big, raggedy brown rug, she announced, "Okay, all you funners, we're going to f-l-y a-w-a-y on this wonderful m-a-g-i-c c-a-r-p-e-t! Everyone come sit down on it so we can get ready to f-l-y!"

Becky wondered if some of the kids might not want to, but Tricia made it sound so mysterious and exciting that the children stopped everything and hurried to sit on the old rug. The last of the mothers smiled as they went through the breezeway gate.

Jess, Cara, and Becky sat down at the picnic table to blow up balloons and crunch foil into small balls for the next game.

Tricia stood in the middle of the raggedy rug, the kids

sitting around her. She wore white shorts and a white T-shirt, and the morning breeze stirred her long, reddish-blond hair, making her look even more dramatic. She also looked determined to hold their attention, even if it killed her.

"Before we go sailing away, my m-a-t-e-y-s, we should know each others' n-a-m-e-s," she told them. "Now, I know we all have name tags, but not all of us can read yet. Let's call out our names and tell how o-l-d we are too."

"Craig Leonard!" yelled the boy who wanted to learn to stand on his hands. "Seven years old!"

"Sam Miller!" called a boy with bright red hair. "Seven." He poked his little red-headed sister, who spoke up, "Sandra Miller! Five years old."

"Wanda Lester. Six," said a shy girl with a brown ponytail.

Her friend, who had a brown ponytail, too, put a hand to her mouth to hide a giggle. "Wendy Johnson. Six."

Jojo and Jimjim Davis yelled, "Umpty-um-la-da-da!"

Tricia looked like she might ask them again, then changed her mind.

Suzanne called out her name and "Seven!" Then Amanda, Sally Lowe, Blake Berenson, and Bryan said their names and "Five!"

"W-e-l-c-o-m-e, m-a-t-e-y-s!" Tricia called out. "Now, everyone hold on to the corners and edges of our m-a-g-i-c c-a-r-p-e-t." Once they'd all grabbed hold, she asked, "Now think very carefully. Where shall we g-o-o-o?"

They all eyed her as if she were weird.

"Over the P-a-c-i-f-i-c O-c-e-a-n?" she asked.

"Yeh!" someone yelled. "Over the ocean!"

Sam Miller said, "I get to be captain."

"I wanna be," Craig Leonard argued.

Tricia shot them a withering glance. "On this c-a-r-p-e-t s-h-i-p, you're all equal, m-a-t-e-y-s. I am Tricia Bennett, your c-a-p-t-a-i-n. No arguing, or the c-a-r-p-e-t cannot take off. Are you r-e-a-d-y?"

They all nodded, holding tightly to the rug's ragged edges.

Tricia flung out an arm. "All mateys close their eyes for take-off. Harrrummm. . . . harrrummm. . . . T-a-k-e o-f-f! Here we go through the air! H-a-n-g o-n!"

Becky had to smile as she sat at the redwood table rolling up foil balls. One thing about Tricia—even on a raggedy old carpet she had a commanding presence. The two of them used to play magic carpet years ago, and Tricia had made it seem real then, too.

"A-h-o-y! I spot the Pacific Ocean in the distance!" Tricia announced. "Quick! Lean to your l-e-f-t," she called out, zooming her outstretched arms to the left. "What's that thing on the b-e-a-c-h?"

"Sand!" someone yelled, making the other funners giggle.

"Palm trees!" Sally Lowe put in.

Tricia intoned, "Sand and palm trees . . . and I do believe s-e-a-w-e-e-d and flocks of s-e-a-g-u-l-l-s. Listen to those sea-gulls caw. Caw . . . caw . . . caw . . ." She zoomed her arms again. "And now we are f-l-y-i-n-g over the Pacific Ocean. Ahoy! What's that huge fish?"

"A whale!" Sam Miller yelled. "A killer whale!"

"A shark! The world's biggest shark!" Craig announced.

"Hold on tight to the carpet!" Tricia warned them. "Hold on with all of your might. A-h-o-y! Ships below. What are they?"

"Submarines," Craig Leonard said.

"Sailboats!" Amanda threw in, no doubt remembering

them from brunch at the Beachcomber restaurant.

Tricia zoomed her arms higher. "And now we f-l-y, f-l-y, f-l-y to Catalina Island for a glass-bottom boat tour of the fish in the d-e-p-t-h-s of the ocean."

"Urga-burga-bof-bof!" the Davis twins yelled wildly. "Urga-burga-bof-a-lof!" Becky hoped that Tricia could keep them busy for a long, long carpet ride. Like the entire morning.

Finally, Tricia brought the magic carpet riders back to Santa Rosita after a dramatic, "P-r-e-p-a-r-e for a bumpy landing—p-r-e-p-a-r-e!" The funners were all laughing happily, when she promised that on Wednesday they'd fly into outer space. The kids were so pleased, they helped roll up the rug so it would be ready for the space flight.

Becky had hung a wooden hoop from the pepper tree. "Now we'll play foil ball toss," she told the funners as they surrounded her. "I'll hand out these foil balls, and we'll see who can toss them into this hoop I've hung from the tree."

They'd no more than lined up under the tree than Sam Miller spotted the tree house up in the branches. "Tree house!" he yelled. "Tree house!"

"We're not going to play in the tree house," Becky announced. "It's too dangerous." She didn't know that for sure, only that if *everyone* climbed up there, it surely would be.

But Sam was already halfway up the tree, and Jojo and Jimjim scrambled up right behind him.

"Out of the tree!" Becky yelled at them. "Out, now!"

Blake Berenson headed straight for the swings.

Tricia yelled, "Out of the tree house, mateys!" But even she couldn't budge them, and she muttered from the corner of her mouth, "Get the others playing the ball toss."

Becky handed out the small foil balls and lined up the kids.

They tossed the balls into the hoop for a while, but they were far more interested in watching Sam, Jojo, and Jimjim above them in the dangerous tree house.

From then on, everything began to go downhill. Even Jess couldn't rally the funners by bouncing balloons in the air. And instead of sitting quietly at the table for mid-morning snacks, everyone ran around the yard, yelling wildly and spilling apple juice on themselves. Raisins and graham crackers were spilled all over the yard.

Finally, Jess's flips and cartwheels and walking on her hands caught their attention. Even Sam climbed down from the tree house to try it, and the twins peered down to watch. But most of the funners could only do somersaults, and after about fifteen minutes all of them except Craig lost interest.

Cara shook her head. "One thing's for sure, I don't ever want to teach little kids! Were we ever like this?"

"That's because you don't have a little sister or brother," Becky said, hoping Cara wouldn't quit. "We'll just have to see what they like to do most. What's left to do are crafts and the sand castle contest. Maybe we should split them into small groups."

Jojo and Jimjim stayed up in the tree house, but the rest of them split up, either making Quack-Quack Duck puppets with Becky, or making sand castles in the sandbox with Cara and Jess.

Becky hadn't thought she'd have to do most of the cutting and gluing for the little kids, and that the older ones would finish quickly. Her head began to ache fiercely, and she wished she could sit in the tree house herself. Whenever Mrs. Bennett appeared at the kitchen window, Becky asked, "What time is it?"

It seemed ten hours had passed when noon finally came and the parents picked up their funners. To Becky's surprise, the kids yelled, "Goodbye, goodbye! We'll come again!"

"Whew! Are little kids crazy or what!" Cara said, flopping down on her back in the grass.

The others flopped down around her, exhausted. Staring up at the sky, Becky yelled, "Ufff! I've got soggy graham crackers in my hair!"

"Those kids were wild!" Jess exclaimed. "And that Jojo and Jimjim and their corny Umpty-dumpty-um-dum-a-lum! It was worse than working at Mrs. Llewellyn's."

Suddenly they were all giggling uncontrollably.

"This is Club El Wacko, all right!" Tricia announced.

Becky laughed till she could hardly breathe, and no one said anything about quitting Morning Fun for Kids.

On the way home, Amanda told Becky, "It was lots of fun."

"Good," Becky said, smiling down at her little sister. "I'm glad you thought so." She was $13.50 richer, but right now she felt sure she didn't ever want to see another funner again.

That is, until she picked up the newspaper and got the mail from the mailbox.

First, the *Santa Rosita Times* had an article about Becky and the Twelve Candles Club. The headline read, LOCAL GIRLS' CLUB USES SUMMER ADS FOR KIDS. There was a picture of them dressed in their cowgirl costumes, with Mr. and Mrs. Llewellyn. The article began:

> Becky Hamilton, Tricia Bennett, Cara Hernandez, and Jess McColl are only a few of the hundreds of students on vacation who have taken advantage of the *Times'* free want ads for kids, which are found in today's paper.
>
> These four enterprising Santa Rosita twelve-year-olds

are available for light housecleaning, party-helping, car and window washing, baby-sitting, and a preschool called Morning Fun for Kids. But these girls are more than just ambitious, they're also generous. When working at the Llewellyn benefit for Casa de Amparo, they donated half their earnings for abused children.

Becky Hamilton also made the news Saturday, when neighborhood dogs chased her as she delivered her hand-made pepperoni pizza party invitations!

Other students. . . .

Becky skimmed the rest of the article. She felt good about it, even though she was tired of hearing about the great pepperoni chase. As for Morning Fun for Kids, they sure couldn't stop—not now that it had been mentioned in the newspaper.

Also in the mail were two other newspapers: the *Omaha World-Herald* and the *Colorado Springs Gazette Telegraph*. Those were two of the cities Mom was considering moving to! Becky thought about hiding the papers in the garbage, but her mother would probably wonder why they hadn't come, and ask.

No matter how awful the funners had behaved, Becky decided she'd rather stick with the kids than move. She just hoped Jess, Cara, and Tricia wouldn't decide to quit. It was one thing to work hard for Mrs. Llewellyn, but quite another to care for wild kids.

"How did Morning Fun for Kids go?" her mother asked when she phoned from the office during her lunch hour.

"I think the kids had fun," Becky told her, "but they almost drove us right out of our minds."

Mom laughed. "Are you going to continue it?"

"Sure," Becky answered, determined. "And guess what? There's an article about us in the *Santa Rosita Times*. I've already gotten calls because of it."

"More job offers?" Mom asked.

"Yes! and Mrs. Davis wants me to baby-sit for her twins tonight from seven till ten. Mrs. Davis was my second-grade teacher."

"Do you really want to, Becky? You've been working so much this week—"

"Sure, I do. The Davis kids are interesting. They have their own secret language, and it seems each knows what the other one is thinking. They're something else."

"Well, if you're certain," Mom said, not sounding too convinced.

"I'm sure," Becky answered. "My only trouble is remembering what I have to do when. There's so much to do."

"We have some free daily planner calendars left here at work. I'll bring one home for each of you," Mom said.

"Do you really think we need them, Mom?" Becky asked.

"I think they might come in handy. What do you have to do today?"

"Well, right now, Amanda and I are eating peanut butter and jelly sandwiches for lunch. I have to make the ten shell cards for Gram's friend's beach party. At four-thirty, we have a TCC meeting at Jess's house. I'll take Amanda with me. And tonight, I baby-sit for the twins."

"Just make a list for today, then check things off when they're done. I think the calendars will make life easier for you when you're so busy," Mom said. "By the way, please put the meatloaf and potatoes in the oven at four-twenty. The instructions are on the pink note on the refrigerator."

"Yeh," Becky said, craning her neck. "I see it."

"If any of you gets a more complicated job, it might be best to divide it up among you."

"Sounds like a good idea, Mom," Becky said.

As soon as she hung up the phone, it rang again. "Oh, no!" Becky was beginning to feel as if she were Mrs. Llewellyn. At the same time, she was glad to get plenty of work. Jobs from the TV interview and the newspaper wouldn't continue to come in forever.

When people asked for help, Becky thought it best to say, "Our Twelve Candles Club will meet at four-thirty this afternoon. May we call you this evening for final arrangements?"

Everyone was agreeable.

After reading a story to Amanda, she settled her down for a nap. Becky wondered if all the funners were as tired as Amanda after their hectic morning.

After slipping two quarters from the Morning Fun for Kids into her mom's coin jar, and the thirteen dollars into the wooden ice bucket, Becky wrote out today's list, then the jobs they needed to discuss at the meeting this afternoon.

Monday

9–12 a.m.	*Morning Fun for Kids*
12–1	*lunch*
1 p.m.	*Put Amanda down for nap*
1–4	*Make shell cards for Gram's friend.*
	Make sample cards for club to sell.
4:20	*Put meatloaf & potatoes in oven.*
4:30–5:30	*TCC Club meeting at Jess's.*
7–10	*Baby-sit Jojo and Jimjim Davis*

111

Housecleaning	Window/Car Washing	Party Help	Baby-sitting
Mrs. O'Lone 577–2623 3 hrs. Tues. or Thurs. (all of us)	Mrs. Zable 577–2390 2 cars & windows Saturday (?)	Kids' party 577–0012 June 15 1–4 (all of us)	Mrs. Davis 577–0987 tonight 7–10 (Becky)
Mrs. Boles 578–2999 3 hrs. Tues. or Thurs. (2 of us)	Mrs. Lieger 590–2524 any day this week (3 or 4 of us)	Mrs. Kyle 590–2337 kid's party June 22 (2 of us)	Mrs. Brown 590–2119 every Wed. 6–9 p.m. 1 girl (8) (1 of us)
Mr. Terhune 590–3231 3 hrs. Sat. (2 of us)	Mrs. Klatt 590–7079 2 cars every Saturday a.m.		

"Whew!" Becky thought. She was glad her mother would be bringing home daily planners. They were going to need them if they were going to remember all these jobs and keep track of who was going to do what all summer long. But it did feel better to have everything written down so the jobs weren't driving her wacko as they raced around in her head.

Next, Becky gathered her supplies for making the shell cards and spread them out on the dining room table to get started. She had sparkle pens, shell and other sealife design stamps, colored stamp pads, colored pencils, and pre-cut, pre-folded index card paper.

First, she pressed the shell stamps on the blue ink pad and stamped the cards. Next, she used the aquamarine and burgundy ink pads for the other sealife design stamps. After that, she highlighted them all with colored pencils and glued on the sparkles. Below the shimmering design, she lettered the words,

IT'S A BEACH PARTY!

And, inside, she carefully wrote,

PLACE:
DATE:
TIME:

In spite of answering a few more phone calls, Becky finished the ten cards and three samples for advertising by four o'clock. Relieved, she checked off "make shell cards for Gram's friend" and "make sample cards for club to sell" from the day's list.

Amanda awoke and came into the kitchen just as Becky was setting places at the kitchen counter for dinner. "You're going to have to come to the Twelve Candles Club meeting with me," Becky said as she placed three napkins and three glasses by the plates.

Amanda's sleepy eyes widened. "You mean I can really go?"

"If you sit quietly and listen," Becky said, since Amanda was so excited about it.

"I will," Amanda promised. "I will!"

At four-twenty, Becky turned on the oven and put in the meatloaf and potatoes. Another job done. Taking her list of jobs for the meeting, she headed for the door. "Come on, Amanda, time to go."

After stopping at Tricia's, the three hurried to Jess's house. Cara arrived from her house across the street just as they did, and they went up the walk and knocked on Jess's door.

"Does Jess have her own outside door?" Amanda asked.

"Sure," Becky said, "it used to be the side door to the garage before they remodeled it into Jess's bedroom and built the new garage next to it."

Jess opened the door. "Come on in."

"Wow!" Amanda exclaimed as she took in the gym equipment and the huge posters.

Jess smiled. "Do you like my bedroom, Amanda?"

Amanda nodded.

"I'll have to bring Amanda, except when she's at Gram's," Becky explained.

"I'll be quiet," Amanda promised before anyone could object.

Jess set an oak desk chair to face the twin beds. "For our president."

Becky laughed, and sat down dutifully while the rest of them plopped onto the twin beds.

"The meeting of the Twelve Candles Club will now come to order. First of all, I'd like to pass out samples of my shell cards in case you would like to take orders for them. I can print anything on the cover and inside. They can be used for invitations, birthday cards, or note cards. They sell for $1.50 each, and Mom thought I should pay you a quarter for each one you sell. What do you think?"

Tricia spoke up, "It's a great idea, Becky. I think they'll sell easily."

"A quarter for each one sold sounds fair enough. You have to buy all the supplies," Jess said.

"Count me in," Cara agreed.

"Oops, I forgot," Becky said. "Is there any old business?"

"I've been getting phone calls from the article and the ads in the *Santa Rosita Times*," Cara answered. "I've gotten five job offers, mostly housecleaning and baby-sitting."

"I've got seven," Tricia said. "One for all four of us to work at a humongous kids' birthday party tomorrow."

"And I had six on the answering machine today," Jess said. "One window washing, one car washing, and the rest house cleaning."

"Whoa!" Becky held up her hand. "I've got ten! That's a total of . . . ummm . . . twenty-eight offers! Did everyone get references?"

They all nodded, and Becky showed the girls how she had listed hers in columns. "We should all probably list the jobs out like this so we can see if anything overlaps. Mom's bringing home some free daily planners from work for us, so we can keep track of what's happening every day."

"That will help a lot," Tricia said, "but we'll still have to make lists like these, too, until we decide who can do what. Whoa! It's going to work fine!"

When they'd finished listing the jobs, dates, and times, they split up the list of names for each to call back. "It really helps to check off jobs when they're done," Becky said. "It makes you feel like you've accomplished something."

The phone rang and Becky said, "It's probably a call from the fliers. We told people to call between four-thirty and five-thirty."

Jess picked up the phone. "Twelve Candles Club." Then she laughed. "Mom! *You* didn't have to call between four-thirty and five-thirty! Yes, I think we can help at your office party. Three Saturdays from now? I'll have to call you back." Jess grinned. "Say, Mom, you could use Becky's shell invitations. I've got a sample! Bye, Mom."

"More business," Tricia said, holding up a hand. "We'd

better all pay up our three dollars to buy snacks for Morning Fun for Kids. I had to use my own money yesterday."

Everyone who had money with them paid up, and Tricia marked the entries in her treasurer's notebook.

Becky looked serious. "The way those kids acted this morning, I wouldn't have blamed you if you'd all quit. It's not fair for all of you to do all this work just so I don't have to move away."

"That's not the only reason," Jess said. "I don't want to quit. Dad's got my three brothers to send to college beginning this fall. Anyhow, I like being able to buy my own leotards and other gymnastics stuff."

"I like making my own money, too," Cara put in, "even if the kids are crazy."

"I could use money for voice lessons this summer," Tricia said. "And I'll need some for acting camp."

"You want to sing, too?" Becky asked.

"Everybody needs voice lessons for acting. For inflections, projecting, foreign accents—there's lots to learn, and voice lessons help."

"Speaking of lots to learn," Becky said, "let's discuss ways to make Morning Fun for Kids easier."

They'd just gotten started when the phone rang again. Cara picked it up. "Twelve Candles Club." Her brown eyes lit up. "Oh, Mrs. Llewellyn. Yes, it's a very nice picture of all of us in today's paper. Every Thursday morning from nine to twelve? No, no, I'm sure she won't."

Becky and the others strained to get the message.

"May I call you back after we've discussed it?" Cara asked. "Okay, just one moment." She put her hand over the receiver. "Mrs. L. wants us to clean for her on Thursdays before we're all booked up. Just until her cleaning lady's well. She's afraid she'll lose us if we wait and call back. She's even offering us pizza for lunch!"

"Every Thursday? Let's go for it," Jess said. "The dishes are already washed and the silverware is polished. Maybe she'll have another party."

"Yeh! Let's do it!" Tricia agreed.

Becky nodded, and Cara spoke again to Mrs. L. "We'll be happy to clean for you, Mrs. Llewellyn. No, we won't let Becky bring any more pepperoni cards to be delivered. Okay, thank you. Bye."

When Cara hung up, everyone burst into laughter.

Becky mocked her disappointment. "No more pepperoni cards?"

Cara collapsed on the floor. "Mrs. L. says—" Cara caught her breath. "Lulu still hasn't recovered from the big chase. She still has bouts of panting!"

Just the memory of it made Becky feel happy about working for Mrs. Llewellyn again, and happier yet that they could work together all summer.

————

That evening, Becky half-dreaded her baby-sitting job for the twins. When Mr. Davis arrived to pick her up, she couldn't believe how much he looked like a grown-up version of his sons. He had dark curly hair, green eyes, and freckles across the bridge of his nose. "I've seen you on TV, and now I've read about you in the newspaper," he said. "You're kind of famous."

Becky felt a blush rise to her cheeks. "Not me! Not famous!"

She buckled up in the car and put her new Ginger book called *Go for It!* on her lap. Maybe she'll have a chance to read when the twins were in bed.

"The boys enjoyed being at your morning preschool," Mr. Davis said as they drove off. "They usually don't care for that kind of thing."

"They liked the tree house the best," Becky commented.

"I'll bet!" Mr. Davis said.

When they arrived at the Davis home, Jojo and Jimjim were at the front door in their Superman pajamas. One of them exclaimed, "Tree house!" and they both smiled broadly. Becky expected to hear some of their secret language, but they didn't use it, at least not yet.

Mrs. Davis gave Becky a list of instructions, then added, "The boys certainly enjoyed this morning. I warned them to behave tonight if they want to attend Morning Fun for Kids again."

Good idea, Becky thought to herself.

"Their *Babar, the Elephant* video is ready to go," Mr. Davis said and showed her the VCR.

Moments after Mr. and Mrs. Davis left, she sat down with the boys to watch *Babar, the Elephant*. As soon as it was over, Jojo and Jimjim said in unison, "Again!"

Becky decided it wasn't too bad, getting paid for watching a video. The boys went to bed without a fuss after three showings of *Babar*. Becky thought it was almost too good to be true and prayed a grateful, "Thank you, Lord." At long last, a rest.

The whole evening was uneventful, until Becky returned home. At the kitchen counter, Mom had been reading the Omaha newspaper.

"Hi, Beck," she said with a forced smile. "Guess what?

I've found some job possibilities in this Omaha paper. I'm wondering if it might be a nice place to live."

Becky stood rooted to the carpet, her heart sinking.

"Honey," her mother began slowly, "I know this is hard for you, but I just don't see any other choice. Please, try to understand . . ." Her tired voice trailed off.

The reality of moving away hit Becky full force. *I'll never see my friends again, and I won't know anyone in a new city. How could Mom do this to me? How can she expect me to be happy about it!*

Anger and frustration washed over her, and she blurted, "No! I don't want to move—I want to stay here! Why are you doing this to us?"

Hurt and disappointment filled her mother's face, and Becky felt terrible for her words.

"Listen, Becky," Mom said, "this is not easy for me, either, but it's our only option. I didn't want to bring it up at dinner, but our car is breaking down, and I don't have enough money to fix it."

Becky's throat tightened. "Oh, Mom, I'm sorry . . . I didn't really mean what I said. I'll try to be happy—" Her voice broke and tears ran down her cheeks.

Her mother held her close, stroking Becky's hair like she did when she was little. "It's going to work out, honey. I know it will." She pulled a tissue from the box and handed it to her. "Now, better get to bed. I glanced at your schedule for to-morrow, and it looks like you have a full day. Gram's taking Amanda, so you won't have to bring her with you."

Becky nodded and trudged toward her bedroom. In the hallway, she made a detour to her mother's bedroom and stuffed half her baby-sitting money into her billfold. It wouldn't buy a car or a washing machine, but it might help.

CHAPTER

9

Becky sat at the kitchen counter and listed the day's jobs in the daily planner her mother had given her:

9–12 A.M. Clean house for Mrs. O'Lone.
1–4 P.M. Birthday party helper for Staci Thurston.
5 P.M. Chicken & rice casserole in oven.

She popped the last bite of a banana into her mouth. So far, the day looked easier than yesterday. It helped a lot that Mom had taken Amanda to Gram's, and at the same time had delivered the ten beach party invitations to her.

Becky headed for the garage door to get her bike. Time to go since Mrs. O'Lone's house was a twenty-minute ride away. As she walked the bike out the side door, Jess, Cara, and Tricia coasted to a stop on the street out front.

"Rise and shine!" Tricia called out.

In spite of feeling discouraged about her mother's car troubles, Becky tried to joke about the housecleaning job ahead. "Especially *shine*," she said, as she hopped onto her bike.

The others laughed, and she rode out to join them. "We're off!" Jess yelled, pedaling down the street again.

"Way off!" Tricia teased. "It's Club El Wacko off to clean up the world!"

Everyone laughed again except Becky. It was good, though, to ride with the breeze in her hair and the sun on her back; and for a moment, she wished she could just keep on riding to a place where she'd never have troubles again.

After a while, Tricia pedaled up alongside her. "What's wrong, Beck?"

Becky took a deep breath. "Mom thinks her car is going to break down and the washing machine died Saturday. Things are getting worse." She felt like crying. "I feel like time is running out."

"I've forgotten to pray for you lately," Tricia admitted, "but, believe me, I will now."

"Thanks," Becky choked out.

"Have you given thanks to God in this situation?" Tricia asked.

"Are you kidding?"

Tricia explained, "Gramps says that giving thanks, in spite of our problems, changes matters in heaven. We don't always know why we are to give thanks, except that God tells us to do it."

A car horn honked behind them, and Tricia sped ahead of Becky. "Sorry!" she yelled to the driver. "But it was important!"

Riding along behind her three best friends, the thought of moving away hurt Becky even more. *What would she do without them?* she wondered. She had to force herself to pray, *Lord, I thank You . . . I thank You in spite of maybe moving away from my friends*. It wasn't an easy prayer, but she wanted to obey God. Maybe better feelings about it would follow, but right now, they didn't.

The O'Lones lived in an old two-story Spanish-style house that overlooked the ocean. The house had lots of nooks and crannies, and peeling paint around the windowpanes. It would be harder to clean than Mrs. Llewellyn's ultra-modern house, or the newer houses in Santa Rosita Estates. "I'll wash the outside windows," Becky offered.

The others looked at her as though she were crazy. At the same time, Becky could tell they were worried about her. "I feel like being outside today, all right?"

"You're on," Jess said. "You can have those windows."

————

Later, as Becky climbed the ladder to the second-floor windows, a heaviness settled over her, and dark thoughts began to pierce her mind. *What if I flung myself from this ladder? I could just let myself fall . . . all my troubles would be over*. The ladder felt wobbly under her feet as the thought sunk in.

Just as quickly, she knew the idea was evil. *Help me, Jesus!* she prayed. *I don't want to think like that! Help me, Jesus!*

Slowly, she began to feel at peace.

As she washed the first window, she began to sing, "Oh, How He Loves You and Me!" a song they'd sung in Sunday school. Singing about God's love raised her spirits as she worked. It helped, too, to be outside and see the beauty of the sky, clouds, and trees. She glanced over the rooftops and tried to imagine sketching the different scenes. *God has given every-*

one at least one talent to use to His glory, she remembered from class. *Thank you, Lord, for giving me a talent for art.*

When they'd finished cleaning and were on their way home, Becky waved her friends on. "I told Mom I'd buy milk and bread," she told them.

"Are you sure you don't want us to come with you?" Tricia asked.

"I'm sure," Becky answered. She didn't like her best friend looking at her so worried.

Once in the supermarket, she added cheese, lunchmeat, crackers, lettuce, and peanut butter to the list. As busy as her mother was, she probably wouldn't notice the extra things in the refrigerator—things Becky had paid for herself.

That afternoon, the Twelve Candles Club all worked at the birthday party for six-year-old Staci Thurston and twenty-two kindergarten classmates. The party was so wild, there was no time for Becky to worry. The kids burst one another's balloons, and instead of pinning the tail on the donkey, they chased one another with thumbtacks, shrieking. Blowing bubbles turned into a game of getting soap in the other kids' eyes, making them wail. In the midst of the chaos, Becky wished she had a referee's whistle. She would have called the party to a halt.

Tricia crossed her eyes, and Cara asked, "How did we ever get into this?"

"Easy," Jess answered. "We advertised to help at parties."

Becky wished she could sketch the scenes. Despite the uproar, it would make some comical pictures. Maybe God saw people that way at times. Becky helped as best she could until the party ended at four o'clock. When the last of the children were gone, Mrs. Thurston said, "I hope this won't discourage you girls from helping me again."

"Oh, no," Cara assured her, always the sensitive one. "It was . . . interesting."

"Interesting?" Jess echoed.

When Becky arrived home, she found another out-of-state newspaper in the mailbox—this one from Topeka, Kansas.

She brought it in with the other mail, trying not to think about it.

It was six o'clock before Mom and Amanda returned home. "We've got a new car!" Amanda announced to Becky as she ran into the kitchen. "Our old car stopped on the way to Gram's, and we almost got into an accident!"

Becky looked confused, and her mother explained as she came in. "It's a rental car. The repairman says ours isn't worth fixing."

"But I thought we couldn't afford—"

"I had to charge it," her mother said, a look of resignation on her face. "I had to drive Gram's car back and forth to work today, and she arranged for the rental to be at her house when I got back from work."

Becky's heart sank. No matter how hard she worked, she knew she'd never be able to make enough money to buy a car. Maybe she should just quit trying.

Just then the phone rang. "You get it," Mom said. "I've had enough phone calls for today."

Becky picked it up, almost expecting more bad news. It was Mrs. McColl. "Can you make us fifty of those shell cards?"

"*Fifty?*" Becky asked. "I mean . . . yes . . . I can."

Like her daughter Jess, Mrs. McColl always got right to the point. "We want 'IT'S AN OUTDOOR BUFFET' on the front, and the usual 'PLACE, DATE, and TIME' inside. I'll need them in a week."

"Fine," Becky answered, knowing she'd need that much time to make them. "I'll start tonight."

"The office will pay you upon delivery," Mrs. McColl said.

When Becky hung up the phone, she told her mother right away. "Mrs. McColl's office wants fifty of my shell cards."

Her mother smiled faintly. "Congratulations." She looked as numb as Becky was beginning to feel.

"Guess I'll start right after supper," Becky said, "but I only have enough card paper left for ten. I'll need more glue and glitter too."

"I'll pick up more supplies tomorrow," her mom offered.

"I've got money for them," Becky said quickly. "I'll get it out now so I don't forget."

"Just leave it on the kitchen counter," Mom said as she started for her bedroom to change from her business suit.

Becky quickly figured out that fifty cards would bring about fifty dollars in profit, after supplies and paying Jess a quarter each for selling them. Fifty dollars was a lot of money, but not much compared to what they needed. Suddenly an idea flashed into Becky's brain—*Mr. Bradshaw . . . yes, Mr. Bradshaw!*

But did she dare do it?

———

The next day, Becky and Amanda were headed to Tricia's house for Morning Fun for Kids. Becky carried a grocery bag full of craft supplies. She'd decided on paper pizzas for the kids to make, so she'd brought paper plates, red poster paint, and red construction paper. Jess was bringing the holey edges of used computer printer paper to snip slantwise to look like cheese pieces.

"When I'm big, I'm going to marry Bryan," Amanda announced good and loud.

"Really?" Becky said. "I guess that would make us related to Tricia's family."

Amanda nodded. "That's right. And Bryan is gonna live a very, very long time . . . lots longer than me."

Becky pressed her lips together to keep them from quivering. Amanda didn't want anyone else she loved dying on her, like Dad had. Well, she couldn't blame Amanda for feeling that way.

They let themselves in through the Bennetts' gate to the breezeway and backyard. Cara and Jess were already there and looked up. "Thought you weren't coming," Jess said. "You're *never* late."

"I couldn't get going this morning," Becky answered. She knew it was more than that. She just didn't feel like hurrying anymore.

"Where's Bryan?" Amanda asked.

"In the house," Tricia answered. "But he's coming out in a minute, so you may as well wait here."

The Bennetts' cat, Butterscotch, sat on her usual perch in the kitchen window shelf. Mrs. Bennett was washing dishes, and greeted Becky and Amanda through the window.

"Today, we're better prepared for the funners," Tricia announced. "As soon as they start to lose interest, we'll split them into groups. If a few of them want to sit in the tree house or play on the swings or in the sandbox, instead of doing the group activity, we let them. Okay?"

"Okay," Becky chorused with Cara and Jess.

"What about skits?" Cara asked.

"Maybe later, when they're not so hyper," Tricia answered.

Car doors began to slam out front, and Jess groaned, "Here they come!"

Becky didn't feel like being the first to greet anyone, so she busied herself laying out craft supplies on the table while Cara went to the gate.

"Does your Mom have a new car?" Tricia asked.

"It's a rental. Our old one conked out."

"Really? What are you going to do?"

Becky shrugged and turned away. Her lips were already trembling, and this was no time to cry.

"Come on, funners," Tricia said in a loud voice, "if you unroll the magic carpet, we can start thinking about our outer-space travel before the rest of them even get here."

Amanda, Bryan, Wanda, Wendy, and Blake rushed over and began to unroll the rug. Watching them, Becky wondered if Amanda even understood about moving. Probably not, because she never mentioned it. She knew they were in trouble, though. And she'd sure miss Bryan.

Before long, all the funners from Monday had arrived and brought two friends: Merilee Dawson and Jason Turner, both six years old. The moment Mrs. Davis left, Jojo and Jimjim ran for the tree house.

"Time for the m-a-g-i-c c-a-r-p-e-t!" Tricia called out. She captured even Jojo and Jimjim's attention, and they turned from the tree and edged over to the raggedy brown carpet. Tricia asked, "And where do you think we're going to ride today?"

"The moon!" Sam answered.

"No! Outer space!" Craig yelled. "And in outer space, it's easy to walk upside-down!"

"We're going to both those places," Tricia answered. "And,

it *is* easier to walk upside-down in outer space."

"Ugga-bugga-bugga-boo!" Jojo and Jimjim shouted together.

The other kids eyed them strangely, so Tricia yelled, "All a-b-o-a-r-d for o-u-t-e-r s-p-a-c-e!" Once she had them on the magic carpet, they forgot everything else.

If only Tricia could keep them there until noon, Becky wished again.

The morning did go better than on Monday. The kids who wanted to do crafts made the paper plate pizzas. The ones who wanted to build sand castles spent the morning in the sandbox. Others sat in cardboard boxes, roaring and "harumming" as they drove cars and airplanes and space ships. And Jojo and Jimjim only stayed up in the tree house half the morning.

The funners seemed calmer today, too. They even seemed genuinely interested in Blake Berenson's two white mice, which he brought to "show and tell." The mice scurried around in their little cage on the shaded corner of the crafts picnic table, not far from the kitchen window shelf, where Butterscotch eyed them hungrily.

Suddenly Becky heard a soft, "Umpty-dumpty-tum-dum-a-lum." Out of the corner of her eye she saw Jojo and Jimjim open the mice's cage. She screamed as the mice raced down the table leg, and Butterscotch leaped from the window, streaking after them.

"The cat's after the mice!" Becky shrieked as she grabbed a plastic bucket from the sandbox and cornered the mice by the fence. "Stop!" she yelled, plopping the bucket over the mice just as Butterscotch was ready to pounce.

At the same time, Tricia grabbed her cat by the scruff of the neck. "Bad cat!"

"Normal cat," Jess corrected.

"Whew!" Becky sighed. "Another second, and Butterscotch would have had mice for lunch."

It happened so fast, Blake hadn't had time to cry, but he looked like he might now.

"Go get the mice's cage," Becky told him. "We'll make sure they're safe."

He stomped off after the cage. "I'm never going to bring them again," he announced.

"Good idea," Becky said. "Maybe we'll have a special day for bringing pets, okay?"

"What day? What day?" the others chorused.

"We'll let you know," Becky told them, wishing she'd kept her mouth shut.

The morning had helped Becky take her mind off other things, but she was glad when noon came.

That afternoon, after Amanda was settled for her nap, Tricia phoned. "Can I come over for a while?"

"Sure," Becky answered, "but I might put you to work."

When Tricia arrived, she sat down at the dining table to help glue glitter on the buffet party invitations. They'd worn white shorts and their matching blue, white, and green T-shirts today, which made Becky feel closer than ever to her best friend, but somehow sadder, too, when she thought of moving.

After a while, Tricia said, "I don't know if I should tell you something or not."

Becky drew a deep breath. "Tell me what?"

Tricia glued more glitter on a shell without looking up. "I overheard our moms on the phone last night. That's how I knew about your car."

"What were they talking about?" Becky asked, her heart sinking again.

"Your mom thinks you should . . . move this summer. You know, so you'll be settled before school starts."

Tears flooded Becky's eyes. "Oh, Trish, I don't want to move! I've been thinking and thinking what to do, and there's only one chance left."

Tricia looked up. "What's that?"

"You won't tell?" Becky asked her.

"I promise."

"Never in all your life?"

"Never in all my life," Tricia vowed.

"Tomorrow morning when we go to work for Mrs. Llewellyn, I'm going early to see Mr. Bradshaw next door."

"And. . . ?"

Becky swallowed, then again. "I'm going to . . . ask him to marry Mom."

"You're not!" Tricia shrieked. "Oh, Beck, no!"

Becky nodded, teary-eyed, but more determined than ever. "I am. It's our *only* chance of not moving away."

CHAPTER

10

It was just after eight-thirty when Becky pedaled her bike down Seaview Boulevard, then up the driveway of the weathered gray shake house. She hoped for two things—that Mr. Bradshaw was home, and that his sons weren't!

Most of last night, she'd practiced what to say. There was one thing in her favor—Mr. Bradshaw was taking Mom to a church supper tonight, which probably meant he still liked her.

Becky parked her bike by the front porch and stared at the house. *I can't believe I'm doing this!* she thought. Sucking in a deep, determined breath, she started up the steps and prayed desperately, *Please help me, Lord! Please help me!*

She rang the doorbell, then stood quaking in her shoes as she heard the bell chime through the house. *Maybe I can still sneak away before they come to the—*

Just then the door opened, and Becky stared up—way

up—at Chris Bradshaw, who was tall, blond, and handsome—and home from college. "Uh . . . hi," she managed. Her voice quivered as she added, "Is your father home?"

"Sure, just a minute." Chris looked as uneasy to see Becky as she felt seeing him. Still, he turned and yelled, "Dad! Someone to see you!"

Someone? Hmmmph!

She hadn't really considered having the three Bradshaw boys as older brothers. But then, they probably wouldn't be too excited about having two sisters who were only twelve and five years old, either.

A moment later Mr. Bradshaw came to the doorway, jolting Becky from her thoughts. His blue-gray eyes widened. "Why, Becky, what a surprise to see you this morning."

"I . . . I have to talk to you about something—private."

He raised his eyebrows slightly. "Well, shall we sit on the porch swing, then?"

Becky glanced around, glad to see that the windows to the house were closed. "Okay."

A bird twittered in the nearby trees, breaking the silence as they walked over to the swing and sat down.

Mr. Bradshaw gave the swing a push with his feet, and Becky cleared her throat. Her voice sounded too formal and stiff as she said, "The Twelve Candles Club is cleaning for Mrs. Llewellyn again this morning, and I . . . thought I'd come early . . . before you started work."

"That was thoughtful of you, Becky."

Suddenly she wished she'd never come up with this crazy idea, but now Mr. Bradshaw was waiting to hear what she had to say. Maybe she could say she'd forgotten what it was, or changed her mind. *No!* she told herself, gathering courage.

132

Finally, she asked, "You like my mom a lot, don't you?"

"Why, yes, I do," he said, looking puzzled. "She's very nice."

"Would you . . . um . . . would you. . . ?"

Mr. Bradshaw looked even more perplexed, and it was all Becky could do to choke out the words, "Would you . . . marry her?"

Mr. Bradshaw was so taken aback that the swing jerked. "I . . . well, you've taken me by surprise, Becky. May I ask why . . . why you're asking?"

Becky shrugged, struggling to hold back the tears. "Because Mom is thinking of selling our house and moving somewhere that doesn't cost so much. I . . . I just thought that if you were thinking of marrying her anyhow, maybe you could ask her before she gets a realtor to sell the house."

"I see," he answered, rubbing his chin and staring at the porch ceiling.

"*Please* don't tell her I talked to you," Becky pleaded. "It's just that I don't know what else to do. I've been working as hard as I can to make some extra money, but first the washing machine broke down, and now the car. We had to rent one. Everything's getting worse, and Mom wants us to move this summer before school starts."

Mr. Bradshaw looked as if he wanted to pat Becky's arm, but she was glad he restrained himself. "Would you . . . uh . . . like me for a stepfather?" he asked.

"I guess. I haven't really thought much about it. I still miss . . . my father a lot." She rushed on, wondering if that were the right thing to say. "But I think I'd like you, the more I got to know you."

Just then Jess, Cara, and Tricia rode into sight on their way to Mrs. Llewellyn's. Becky edged off the swing. "I'd better get to work. My friends are here."

"I appreciate your stopping by, Becky, and being honest with me," Mr. Bradshaw said, rising to his feet. "I'll give your suggestion some serious thought. I can't say I haven't thought of it myself."

For an instant, Becky's hopes rose, even though he didn't say he'd ask her mother right away. At least he looked like he was interested. "You won't tell Mom I asked you?"

"Of course not. You have my word on that."

She lifted her chin to look brave. "Thanks." But the moment she turned away, tears filled her eyes.

———

That night, when Mr. Bradshaw arrived to pick up her mother, Becky sat at the dining table, working on her buffet party invitations.

"Flowers for a lovely lady," he said, bowing slightly and handing Mrs. Hamilton a beautiful bouquet.

"Oh, Paul, you shouldn't have," Mrs. Hamilton protested, looking flushed. "But I do love flowers." She hurried to put them in a vase with water, then set them on the coffee table in the living room.

Becky thought her mom looked nice, even in her old white dress. Mr. Bradshaw looked like he thought so, too, making Becky feel hopeful again. She kept gluing glitter on a card, not knowing what to say. Fortunately, Amanda burst into the room with Buster Rabbit. "Who are those flowers for?" she asked.

"I brought them for your mother, but you girls can enjoy them, too," Mr. Bradshaw said.

"Wow!" Amanda said. Then speaking to her rabbit, she

added, "You can look at the flowers, but you can't eat them!"

Everyone laughed, and Mr. Bradshaw winked at Becky.

Her spirits soared. Maybe he was going to ask Mom tonight to marry him!

After Amanda was tucked into bed, Becky could hardly concentrate on her work. Her thoughts were filled with how and when Mr. Bradshaw would ask her mother to marry him.

The thought suddenly struck her that her mother might say no, when the phone rang. It was Gram. "I've been missing you since Sunday," she said. "I just felt I should call. I don't like to pry, Becky, but how is everything going?"

"Oh, Gram, I'm glad you asked. Please pray!"

"What about, dear? Is there something wrong?"

"I think Mr. Bradshaw might ask Mom to marry him tonight."

"Oh, what makes you think that?" Gram asked.

Becky blurted, "Because I went to his house this morning and asked him to!"

"You asked him to propose to your mother?! Rebecca Anne Hamilton, you didn't!"

Becky swallowed hard. "I didn't know what else to do, Gram! I've been working as hard as I can, but everything is getting worse instead of better. You know the washing machine broke down, and then the car. Now Mom's talking about the high property taxes here. She wants to move before the end of the summer, so we can get settled somewhere before school starts."

A sob escaped her throat. "I don't *want* to move away from you and my friends, Gram! I don't want to go anywhere! I want to stay right here!"

"Don't cry, dear . . . please," Gram said. "I don't want

you to move, either. I've tried to talk your mother into letting me help, but you know how stubborn she can be." Gram was quiet for a moment. "I can't believe you actually asked Paul Bradshaw to propose marriage to your mother! You've certainly brought matters to a head."

"Please don't tell Mom," Becky begged. She wiped her nose with a tissue. "She would never understand."

"I won't tell her, or anyone," Gram promised. "I know you meant well, and Mr. Bradshaw is a fine man. We'll just have to wait and see what will come of it."

"He brought her flowers tonight. They're at the church supper. Maybe he's asking her right now. I don't even know if I really want her to marry him." Another sob caught in Becky's throat. "I just don't want to move away!"

"Don't cry, dear. Just pray for God's will to be done in the whole matter," Gram said, trying to cheer her. Finally she said, "I'm dying to know what happens tonight."

"I'll call you tomorrow, before we leave for Morning Fun for Kids," Becky offered.

"Please do," Gram said. "Good-night, dear."

It seemed like hours that Becky sat working on the party invitations—stamping on the patterns, penciling in color, then adding the glitter. All the while she thought about the Bradshaw boys as stepbrothers, and Mr. Bradshaw as her stepfather. The whole thing made her nervous. Why had she ever suggested such a crazy idea?

At long last, she heard a car pull up out front. She ached to peek out the kitchen window, but forced herself to stay put at the table, working on the cards.

Then she heard a key in the lock, and her mother stepped quietly into the house—alone. "Why, Becky, you're still up."

"I—I'm working on these cards. I want to get them done early in case there are more orders." She watched her mother carefully, hoping she'd look different or something. But she only pulled off her high-heeled shoes and headed for her bedroom.

Becky asked quickly, "Did you have a good time?"

Her mother answered, "Yes, we did. We had a good time."

"Did he . . . did anything exciting happen?"

Her mother stepped back into the dining room. "What do you mean by that, Becky?"

"I thought maybe . . . you know, he'd want . . ." the words slipped from her lips before she could catch them, ". . . to get married or something."

Her mother's mouth dropped open. "What do you mean? Did you put him up to it, Rebecca?"

Becky bit down on her lips. "I . . . uh—"

"Rebecca!" her mother said, shocked. "You didn't!"

Becky slumped down in her chair. "I . . . I just did it because I didn't want to move, Mom. I thought if he was going to ask you anyway, he might as well do it before you got a realtor—"

"I can't believe you'd do such a thing!" her mother said, sounding angry. "This is something between Mr. Bradshaw and me. It is none of your business. Can't you understand that?"

Becky felt ashamed and embarrassed. "I only wanted to help, Mom! Besides, Mr. Bradshaw said he'd been thinking about asking you to marry him anyhow."

Mom shook her head. "I suppose you meant well. But you must never meddle in such things again. Do you understand?"

"Yes!" Becky said, her heart pounding hard. "I promise

I'll never do anything like that again."

"I have another question for you," her mother said, "Have you been slipping extra bills into the ice bucket, and my wallet?"

"Uh—" Becky began.

"The coin jar looks suspiciously full, too," she added.

"I thought if I helped with expenses, we wouldn't have to move."

"I see," Mrs. Hamilton said, looking close to tears herself.

"Mom, what did you say to Mr. Bradshaw, tonight?"

Her mother closed her eyes and drew a deep breath. "I told him I was honored that he would ask, but that I wasn't ready to marry anyone yet. I—I'm still in love with your father, Becky."

Becky's lips trembled. "Oh, Mom, I still love him, too! It was awfully hard for me to bring it up to Mr. Bradshaw—because of Dad, I mean. And I didn't know about having his boys for stepbrothers, either."

Mrs. Hamilton smiled and drew Becky up from the table and into her arms. "We're going to manage, Becky. Whether it's here or somewhere else. It was very tempting to say yes to Paul, but it's wrong to marry someone just to escape your troubles."

"I guess so," Becky agreed.

It felt good to be held in her mother's arms, but the hurt didn't disappear.

————

The next morning, Becky phoned Gram as soon as her mother left for work.

"What happened?" Gram asked.

"Mom loves Dad too much to get married again."

Gram didn't answer, and Becky added, "I'm kind of glad. I wasn't so sure about it."

"Well, I know what I'll be doing today," Gram murmured, almost to herself. "I've got to run, dear."

As usual, Morning Fun for Kids was so hectic that Becky scarcely had a chance to think of her problems. Except once, when Tricia whispered, "What happened last night?"

Becky only shook her head sadly.

After they were home and had lunch, Becky read to Amanda and put her down for a nap.

"You look very sad," Amanda said. "Do you want to hold Buster Rabbit?"

"No, thanks," Becky answered. She trudged to the dining table to work on her cards again. After a while, she heard the mail truck outside, and she looked at her watch. It was Friday, and the delivery was late, as usual. Becky went out to the mailbox, just as Tricia came out for their mail.

"What happened with your mom last night?" Tricia asked.

"Mom still loves Dad too much. She says it's wrong to marry someone just to escape your troubles."

"I guess so," Tricia said. "But I still want you to stay here."

Becky took the mail from the box. "Me too." She sorted through the junk mail. "Hey, here's a letter for me from church. It's from Bear . . ."

Tricia hurried over to look at the envelope. "Wonder what that's about."

Becky tore open the envelope, and they read the letter together:

Dear Becky,
    I've been praying for you, and thought you might like
to have the enclosed guidelines for prayer. They've helped

a lot of people, and I thought they might help you. In the meantime, I'll continue to pray for you.

With Jesus' love,
Bear

Becky looked at the attached sheet. Across the top it read: *"These biblical guidelines will help you to pray more effectively—and experience greater results."*

"Exactly what we need," Becky said. "Greater results."

She read the first guideline aloud. "Join together in prayer with other believers. 'If two of you on earth agree about anything you ask for, it will be done for you by my Father in heaven. For where two or three come together in my name, there am I with them.' Matthew 18:19."

"That means Jesus is with us when we pray together," Tricia said. "Let's go sit on your front step and pray right now."

She and Tricia had never prayed together before, and Becky felt a little uneasy. They settled down on the step and she read on, "Submit to God with your whole being. 'Humble yourselves, therefore, under God's mighty hand, that He may lift you up in due time.' 1 Peter 5:6."

Becky closed her eyes. "I submit to you, God. I know You're the only one who can help me."

Opening her eyes, she read on aloud, "Believe God will hear and answer."

"I believe that," Tricia said.

"I do, too," Becky agreed.

She read again: "Do battle in the spiritual realm. Ephesians 6:12 says, 'For our struggle is not against flesh and blood, but against the rulers, against the authorities, against the powers of this dark world and against the spiritual forces of evil in heavenly realms.' " She turned to Tricia. "How do you do battle?"

Tricia took a deep breath. "My grandfather says we have to cast Satan out of a situation, in Jesus' name." She closed her eyes and said in a strong voice, "And that's what I do now. Satan, get out of Becky's life and her family's life. Leave them alone, in Jesus' name!"

"Amen!" Becky added loudly, then read on, "Listen to the voice of the Holy Spirit. First Corinthians 2:9, 10 says, 'However, as it is written: "No eye has seen, no ear has heard, no mind has conceived what God has prepared for those who love Him"—but God has revealed it to us by His Spirit.' "

The two sat quietly for a long time. There was only the twittering of birds in the trees, and the sound of a car in the street. They couldn't say that they'd *heard* the Holy Spirit speaking, but Becky began to feel the sadness disappear from her heart and peace flood in. "I think something wonderful is going to happen," she told Tricia. "I really *believe* it!"

She read on, "Ask God for what you want! 'I will do whatever you ask in my name, so that the Son may bring glory to the Father. You may ask me for anything in my name, and I will do it.' John 14:13, 14."

"Let's ask," Tricia said quietly, bowing her head.

Becky folded her hands and closed her eyes. "Lord, I ask that we will be able to stay in Santa Rosita, in the name of Jesus." As the words came from her mouth, somehow they no longer seemed so important. "Lord, I guess it'll be fine with me wherever we live. It doesn't matter so much anymore. You'll be with us anywhere we are. I know that for sure."

Tricia shot her a weird look.

Becky read the last step: "Persist until the answer comes."

"That means keep on praying," Tricia said.

Becky nodded, but she had a strange feeling that something had already changed.

———

At six o'clock, Becky and Amanda sat out on the front step with Lass, their dog, waiting for Mom to come home. "Here comes Gram," Amanda said as the familiar green Oldsmobile came down the street.

Becky peered at the car. "That's Mom driving Gram's car!"

Lass barked, and all three ran out to meet her.

Instead of stopping, she just waved, pushed the garage door opener, and drove into the garage. When she stepped out of the car, she sounded excited. "You'll never believe what's happened!"

Was she going to marry Mr. Bradshaw after all? Becky wondered.

"What?" she and Amanda asked together.

"Remember, Becky, when you told me you were going to work as hard as you could in the Twelve Candles Club, because I was working as hard as I could?"

"I guess so."

"Well, I wasn't working as hard as I could," her mother confessed. "Sunday I told you and Gram about a job opening as an account executive."

Becky nodded, wondering what her mother was up to.

"Well, I applied for the job on Monday. I thought maybe I could handle a more difficult job. Just the fact that you've been working so hard helped me gain confidence. Then when I told you how to plan your days and write down your schedule, that helped too. At first, I was afraid they would never consider me for the job, but this afternoon they told me I had it."

"Around two o'clock?"

"Yes, I think it was about two. How did you know?"

"That's when Tricia and I prayed!"

Mom beamed. "Oh, Becky, thank you! It's a miracle! But you set the example for me by working so hard."

Becky's head was in a whirl, trying to take it all in. "What about Gram's car?"

"When I arrived at Gram's, I found she'd bought a brand new car for herself. She insisted on giving me her old one. In fact, she said if I didn't take it, she'd deed it over to you girls. I'm afraid your grandmother is as stubborn as I am. Finally she gave in, and said I could pay for it little by little, but the money is going into savings for college for you two."

"That's Gram, all right!" Becky said. "Whoa—does this mean we get to stay in Santa Rosita?"

Mom's eyes twinkled. "I think so. We won't be rich, but we'll manage if we're careful."

Becky jumped up and down she was so happy. "And I can keep on working in the Twelve Candles Club?"

"It helps a lot if you buy some of your own things," her mother answered.

"Remember when I blew out the candles on my birthday cake? You were all singing 'Happy Birthday' when the idea for the club came to me. When I blew out the candles, instead of a wish, I prayed, *Please help us not to have to move!* I knew then that I had to work as hard as I could."

Mrs. Hamilton gave both of her girls a big hug.

Becky remembered something else. "That wacko dog chase led to the TV and newspaper articles, and then to all the jobs . . . and finally, in a way, to your new job, too."

"I guess you dogs are all right," Mrs. Hamilton said, rubbing Lass's neck.

"Can I tell Tricia and the others?" Becky asked.

"Of course you *may*," her mother corrected, picking up Amanda and whirling her around in the air.

Becky laughed. Grammar was the absolute least of her concerns right now. She ran over to the Bennetts', yelling up at Tricia's open window. "Trish! Trish! We're staying!"

Tricia's head popped out. First surprise showed on her face, then excitement. "Wait, I'm coming down!"

When Tricia came flying out of the front door, Becky shouted, "We really and truly are staying, and mostly because we prayed! And because of the Twelve Candles Club, too."

Tricia's mouth fell open, but not for long. She flung her arms up like a cheerleader. "Thank you, Lord! Thank you for the Twelve Candles Club!"

Becky flung her arms up, too. "Thank you! Oh, thank you, Lord!"

Together, almost as if they'd planned it, Becky and Tricia joined hands in the air and cheered, "Yea! Three cheers for giving us the Twelve Candles Club!"

It seemed that the excitement God had planned for them had only begun.